The Winds of March

A Katie Rose Story

THE WINDS
OF MARCH

by Lenora Mattingly Weber

Image Cascade Publishing

Books by Lenora Mattingly Weber

BEANY MALONE SERIES

Meet the Malones 1943

Beany Malone 1948

Leave It to Beany! 1950

Beany and the Beckoning Road 1952

Beany has a Secret Life 1955

Make a Wish for Me 1956

Happy Birthday, Dear Beany 1957

The More the Merrier 1958

A Bright Star Falls 1959

Welcome Stranger 1960

Pick a New Dream 1961

Tarry Awhile 1962

Something Borrowed, Something Blue 1963

Come Back, Wherever You Are 1969

The Beany Malone Cookbook 1972

KATIE ROSE BELFORD SERIES

Don't Call Me Katie Rose 1964

The Winds of March 1965

A New and Different Summer 1966

I Met a Boy I Used to Know 1967

Angel in Heavy Shoes 1968

STACY BELFORD SERIES

How Long is Always? 1970

Hello, My Love, Good-bye 1971

Sometimes a Stranger 1972

NON-SERIES BOOKS

Wind on the Prairie 1929

The Gypsy Bridle 1930

Podgy and Sally, Co-eds 1930

A Wish in the Dark 1931

Mr. Gold and Her Neighborhood House 1933

Rocking Chair Ranch 1936

Happy Landing 1941

Sing for Your Supper 1941

Riding High 1946

My True Love Waits 1953

For Goodness Sake! (cookbook), with Greta Hilb, 1964

MANUFACTURED IN THE UNITED STATES
OF AMERICA

A hardcover edition of this book was originally published
by Thomas Y. Crowell Company. It is here reprinted by
arrangement with HarperCollins Publishers, New York.

First *Image Cascade Publishing* edition published 2000.
Copyright renewed © 1993 by David Weber

Library of Congress Cataloging in Publication Data
Weber, Lenora Mattingly, 1895–1971.
    The Winds of March.

(Juvenile Girls)
Reprint. Originally published: New York: Thomas Y.
Crowell, 1965.

ISBN 1-930009-11-9 (Pbk.)

TO MY SISTER HELEN

I

Katie Rose Belford, her weight of books clutched to her midriff, walked into study hall at John Quincy Adams High.

This Monday, the first of March, was a bright, sunny day after February's bleak and icy ones. That was why Katie Rose had donned her very best purple jumper with its ruffled blouse the color of violets. Well, the bright sun had prompted her wearing it, along with the knowledge that someone would surely say, "Your eyes look so purple when you wear that outfit." She had still another reason. The tryouts for the musical comedy were due to start any day, and it behooved a girl who was hopeful for a part to look her best.

She and the tall, lanky boy who had walked with her from the lunchroom stopped at their seats. As always, they glanced at the near-by west window to see if the sun were shining, and just how far it was reaching in.

"Miguel, I wish you'd look. It's almost touching the globe on the table today."

Miguel reached out and pushed the world globe closer toward the window. "There now, Petunia, the sun can warm Antarctica. And all the little baby seals can come out of the ice and play, and all the mama seals will say, 'March is coming in like a lamb so that means it'll go out like a lion.' "

Katie Rose giggled. At least three teachers had quoted that to them today.

Mr. Jacoby, their young study hall teacher, turned his spectacled eyes their way. As always, when a teacher glanced toward him, Miguel began tucking in his shirttails. On his gaunt form the shirt refused to stay tucked, just as his straw-colored hair refused to stay parted.

Miguel was really Michael Parnell. But he had come up from Mexico to enter school in Denver, and was listed as Miguel on his transcript, so that was what the student body and faculty called him.

The final bell was clanging when Jeanie Kincaid came hurrying down the aisle and dropped into her seat beside Katie Rose. "I got enough manuscript paper for you and Miguel," she breathed out. "Had to race up to journalism for it."

Katie Rose answered in an almost soundless voice and without moving her lips, "Thanks. Now I can start the story of my life."

Jeanie's cinnamon brown eyes twinkled. " 'I Was a Teenage Goose Girl,' " she said.

Jeanie's hair was the same cinnamon brown as her eyes. She was small and pixielike, but with a great capacity for understanding. Katie Rose often marveled at the way she could say a whole paragraph with one knowing look.

Mr. Jacoby at his desk was now checking over the pupils in study hall with his seating chart. Behind Katie Rose came an admonitory whisper from Miguel, "Don't move, Petunia. I'm trying to finish my apple."

Mr. Jacoby, who was also her lit teacher, had given his classes the autobiography assignment. She got out her ball-point pen and pulled the paper to her, hearing the soft crunch of apple behind her. She was careful not to bend over her desk as she started the story of her life.

"I am sixteen years old, and the second in a family of six children. My brother Ben is a year and a half older than—"

She turned ever so slightly to ask in that same ventriloquist manner without a visible moving of lips,

"Miguel, is it correct to say 'older than me' or—?"

" 'I,' " he said promptly. Miguel might be zany, but he was an authority on when to use *I* or *me, shall* or *will.* Perhaps it was because his father was a writer. He was in Alaska now gathering research for a book while Miguel lived with his grandparents.

Katie Rose glanced up at Mr. Jacoby's sallow face. He had his sarcastic moments as well as his serious ones. "Be honest in writing about yourself," he had urged.

Oh, but you couldn't be honest enough to write, "I hate being poor and having to wear hand-me-downs, and not having money to buy lunches. Nearly all my friends live in new ranch houses in Harmony Heights, and I hate living in an old two-story brick in Hodge-podge Hollow. I wish Mom didn't have to play the piano at a Gay Nineties place to support us since Dad died—"

Mr. Jacoby's crisp voice sounded through the room, "Miguel, now that you're down to the core, would you mind dropping it into the wastebasket? It worries me the way you usually consume them."

A titter rippled through study hall. Oh dear, Katie Rose hadn't done a perfect job of covering for the apple-muncher behind her. Miguel, with a sheepish grin, walked up to the desk, and the core went into the basket with a soft thud.

Katie Rose opened her Prose and Poetry book to consult Mr. Jacoby's reminders. She found another reminder in her mother's hurried scrawl: "Four pounds stewing beef, celery, horse-radish—"

Mother had said at breakfast this morning, "A good old Mulligan stew would taste good tonight. Now who's coming home right after school?"

Not Ben. He wanted to stay on in biology lab. Katie Rose's younger sister Stacy had said reprovingly, "Mom, you know it's always basketball practice at St. Jude's on Monday." So Mother said, "Then Katie Rose love, you stop at Wetzel's." And bossy old Ben had added, "Don't be dawdling around. Get right home so it'll cook in time."

Mr. Jacoby's suggestions were headed:

"Remember that names and dates are boring. Let me see your family."

She wrote:

"My mother's name was Rose O'Byrne before she was married, and all the O'Byrnes are redheaded. I am the only one in my family with black hair. I take after the Belford, or English side of the family."

She looked up as the door opened and a boy, glancing neither to the right nor left, walked up to Mr. Jacoby behind his desk. Katie Rose's heart did a queer fluttery-whish under her violet blouse. Jeanie Kincaid turned and winked roguishly. "Fancy that! Your onetime Mr. Irresistible in person."

Katie Rose winked back. "*Onetime* is right," she muttered. But her eyes noted how his broad shoulders filled out his yellow football sweater, and how his dark hair made a thick curly mat on his head.

He had not only been Mr. Irresistible but the conquering hero and lord of creation all rolled into one. From September to December. How she had basked in his dazzling smile when it was turned on her. How she had ached over him, grateful for any little crumb he tossed her way. And then at Christmas, when it was quite evident she was *not* Miss Irresistible to him, she had taken herself in hand. She had vowed grimly, "I do hereby resolve to shove Bruce Seerie into a storeroom in my heart, and go about business as usual."

She had done just that all through January and February. Today she watched him with only an echo of all the ecstasy and anguish she had known. He spoke to Mr. Jacoby. The teacher nodded briefly. An unsmiling Bruce departed. But she couldn't help wondering if he had seen her among the study-hallers and noticed that her ruffled blouse turned her eyes violet.

She couldn't help wondering why he looked so unhappy. Well, Bruce Seerie's happiness or unhappiness was no concern of hers. *She* had the story of her life to write:

"We have an awful lot of O'Byrne relatives living in the little town of Bannon. The only relatives on my father's side are Grandfather Belford and Aunt Eustace. She travels a great deal. They live within walking distance of us in a huge stone house which is referred to as the Belford mansion."

Another suggestion on Mr. Jacoby's mimeographed page was:

"Tell of your darkest days, and your brightest."

Her darkest days—those despairing days of unrequited love for Bruce Seerie, her longing to be his girl—thank heaven, those were behind her. Her brightest days were ahead of her. Hadn't the drama teacher praised her singing and dancing? Hadn't the dear lady all but promised her a part in the musical comedy that would be put on next month? Katie Rose might even have her tryout sixth hour. A shiver of anticipation passed through her.

The bell rang, and Katie Rose shuffled her pages together and slid them into her large and accommodating Prose and Poetry book. She walked out with Miguel and Jeanie. Each went his separate way to the next class.

At school's end, Katie Rose waited at the first-floor locker she shared with Jeanie. The school day was never properly ended unless they walked out together, and rehashed all its happenings. Katie Rose wanted to tell her that Mrs. Dujardin, their drama teacher, had gone home sick. There had been no talk of the upcoming show or when tryouts would start. Instead, Howard, president of the drama club and Mrs. Dujardin's helper, had led a spiritless discussion of an Ibsen play.

Jeanie must be detained in journalism. Katie Rose waited through all the noisy stampede in the hall while lockers opened and banged shut on all sides of her. The halls quieted somewhat. Then the music students, encumbered with heavy instruments, came clattering down the stairs.

Katie Rose dawdled at her locker. She was looking in the mirror on the inside of the door and applying lipstick though lipstick seemed pretty pointless when her only stop was to be at Wetzel's store. Her heart suddenly set up its uneven fluttery-whish again.

The principal's office was some fifteen or eighteen feet down the hall from this row of lockers. In the mirror she saw the office door open and a small knot of people emerge. Bruce Seerie was among them. So was the ruddy-faced, stocky Adams coach. He had the air of a man who has been dragged into something not to his liking and, after jerky good-bys, he went hurrying off toward the gym. Mr. Jacoby was there too. Katie Rose had never seen him look so grim and uncompromising. Without a ghost of a smile for anyone he, too, walked—or rather, stalked—away.

That left Mr. Knight, their kindly, boyish principal, with a very morose and defiant Bruce, and the woman Katie Rose recognized as his mother. Katie Rose shifted so she could get a better view of her in the mirror. She was a small, compact, no-nonsense type of woman. Jeanie had once told Katie Rose that Mrs. Seerie was the kind to be president of every club she belonged to. The gavel-wielder was pulling on black gloves, and looking very smart in her black dress and short fur jacket.

Mr. Knight kept on talking earnestly to Bruce with his hand on his shoulder. And then he must have been called back to the office for, with a final fatherly and concerned pat, he excused himself.

That left only Bruce and his mother. Katie Rose pretended to be sorting over books as they came her way. They were opposite her when Mrs. Seerie glanced at her watch, and said she'd have to hurry or she'd be late to a committee meeting. She gave Bruce a tight-lipped look which Katie Rose recognized—that This-is-for-your-own-good look. Her heels tapped a determined click as she walked past the lockers and out the door.

That left only Bruce.

He had always been so debonair, so easy-to-smile, so sure of himself and his place in the sun—his place in the sun being on first-string football, the apparatus gym team, and star forward in basketball. His face was dark and fierce as he walked toward her. He said on a down-twisted smile, "Hi, Katie Rose. I have just been kicked off the basketball team."

"Oh no, Bruce! Why?"

"Because that old maid of a Jacoby failed me in lit. That bilious little toad."

So that was what the session was about!

"But can't you make up your assignments? And if you do, he'll sign you up, won't he?"

He said in a bitter monotone, "I've done over my book report on *The Old Man and the Sea* twice, and both times he's banged it back at me with some of his choice sarcasm. I'm supposed to find some important life message in it. This guy that wrote it—"

"Hemingway. He's dead now."

"Yeh, well he didn't die soon enough."

Katie Rose clasped her load of books tight to her. She was suddenly glad Jeanie had been detained in journalism. Jeanie had known Bruce from childhood. They had even dated in desultory fashion before Jeanie decided she liked Katie Rose's redheaded brother Ben.

Oh yes, she was glad Jeanie wasn't here to say, "Too bad, Bruce. Come on, Katie Rose." For it had been Jeanie who advised, "Look, goose girl, as long as you're making no headway with Brucie-boy, why don't you just shove him into a storeroom, and go about business as usual?"

"That's exactly what I'm going to do," Katie Rose had vowed with vehemence.

But this was different. Any girl with school spirit would realize that Adams High needed their best basket shooter, and that the basket shooter needed help to get Mr. Jacoby's signature on his eligible-to-play slip.

Katie Rose said around a catch in her throat, "Bruce, it helps a lot to talk over a book with someone—I mean it clears up things. When Dad was alive he used to read books to us. I got A on *The Old Man and*—because Dad—I was only twelve then—explained the hidden symbolism—you know what Jacoby calls the 'depth charge.' And I—if you'd like me to help you—"

For the first time his gloom and bitterness lifted. "Would you, Katie Rose? Gosh, that'd be swell.

You're so good in all that stuff Jacoby dishes out—
and I'm in such a hole." And then he said the words
she had hungered to hear all through September, Oc-
tober, November, and most of December, "How
about us driving down to Downey's Drug for a
coke?"

Downey's Drug on the Boulevard had a fountain and three booths. The hurried or the unpaired sat on stools at the fountain. Katie Rose and Bruce sat in the corner booth.

This bitterness in Bruce was something different. Always before he'd been so pleased with the world. Through two cokes and the start of a third he vented his spleen. About his parents, and Mr. Knight, the principal. Even the coach who should have gone to bat for him. But mostly it was toward Mr. Jacoby. Old dried-up prune. Not an ounce of school spirit. He had delighted in making it tough for the players all through the football season. Yeh, and he bet that right now the old ghoul was chuckling up his sleeve. Bruce hoped he came down with that virus that was laying so many low.

They were interrupted on that. Downey's helper was an Adams student who was in Katie Rose's drama class. He came over to their table to contribute, "That's what we think Mrs. Dujardin went home with, Katie Rose. A virus."

"Oh no. Just when she was going to start the tryouts."

When their interrupter was called back to the fountain, Katie Rose briefed Bruce on all the points in *The Old Man and*—that had earned her an A. "So, Bruce, you write your report over and let me see it before you turn it in. We'll get it so good Jacoby won't slam it back."

"You're swell, Katie Rose. You're the smartest girl I know."

Bruce's gratitude, his looking up to her was something new too. Always before she had been the grateful, the looking-up-to one. She couldn't help wanting to impress him. She began to talk about other books on their reading list.

Mrs. Downey came over to their table. Heavens, couldn't a girl have any privacy? The druggist's wife was holding out two bottles of instant shoe dye. "Katie Rose, which one of these do you think would match your mother's periwinkle dress? My, it's been years since I've heard of periwinkle blue." At Katie

Rose's blank expression, she added, "You know that lovely old satin dress that Miguel's grandmother found in her trunk, and gave your mother? She wants to dye some white slippers to match."

Why couldn't Mrs. Downey realize that Bruce wasn't just an ordinary coke date? And why did everyone in this part of town have to be so interested in the Belfords? She stole a glance at Bruce. He looked politely bored.

Now if it were Miguel, he'd say, "Let's take both bottles down and try them with the dress—you won't mind, will you, Mrs. Downey?" Yes, and he'd swab the dye on the slippers. It was Miguel who had come into the Belford house bearing this dress that his grandmother—or maybe her mother—had once worn. Miguel had insisted on Mother's trying it on. It was a trifle large around the waist for her, and Miguel had said, "But you can take up some darts or tucks, can't you?" He was always avidly interested in doing for others.

Bruce Seerie was different. Jeanie Kincaid had once pointed out to Katie Rose the Seerie split-level house in Harmony Heights. "Five bedrooms, three baths, game room, patio; and swimming pool shared by the other two neighbors in the circle," she had catalogued. Somehow Bruce wasn't the kind to be drawn into a discussion of the old-time garb Mother wore while entertaining out at Guido's Supper Club—Giddy's Gay Nineties, everyone called it.

She was most vague in her murmured, "I don't really know, Mrs. Downey," and turned back to Bruce to ask him if he had to read *Hiawatha*.

He nodded gloomily. Still smarting under his blow from fate, he spoke of their basketball schedule. He was no braggart but his very wretchedness evidently prompted his, "Coach always counted on my making the free throws."

The door banged open and a noisy whirlwind entered. Oh no, Katie Rose thought—Oh no! These unkempt three were the youngest Belfords who were always lumped as "the littles" in the family. Matt and Jill, the sixth-graders, were twins, and Brian was a year younger. But they were all of a size, all had slate-blue eyes and hair the color of corn flakes. It would take a second look at the three with their identical T-shirts, jeans, and haircuts to see that one was a girl. Katie Rose knew that their three bicycles were leaning against the side of the building outside. Boys' bikes. Jill wouldn't be caught dead riding a girl's.

Today, you'd have thought they were messengers from Garcia. Jill bore aloft a small swatch of the periwinkle satin, and Matt was waving a bill. Brian, who had better manners than the twins, smiled at Mrs.

Downey and said, "Mother said to tell you she appreciated your ordering the colored dye for her."

Katie Rose felt a faint hope that they would complete their purchase and depart without seeing her.

Leave it to Jill not only to see her but to bellow out, "Katie Rose, there you are. Mom's been waiting and waiting for you to come home with the Mulligan stew."

And Matt, not to be outdone, shouted, "She said it ought've been on an hour ago."

Only little Brian flashed her his sober, loving smile. "Maybe it won't take awful long if the meat's cut up in real little pieces."

Wouldn't you know it'd be Mulligan stew tonight! She doubted if such prosaic fare was ever on the menu at the Seerie house.

Bruce said, "I shouldn't have kept you so long, Katie Rose. I'll take you wherever you have to go."

"Just to Wetzel's store. It's not far. We'd better go." She couldn't help feeling apologetic for those rowdy three.

Bruce helped her into the cream-colored convertible, and she guided him to Wetzel's neighborhood store. Funny, how many things in her life she felt slightly apologetic for when she was with Bruce. Even Wetzel's, when he stopped in front of it and said in surprise, "Is this a store? Looks more like a house."

He was evidently thinking in terms of supermarkets. Wetzel's couldn't help looking like a house because it was a one-story frame with its front rooms turned into a store. Customers walked up steps to a porch, and through a door with a tinkling bell that summoned either the limping Mr. Wetzel or his garrulous wife from their living quarters in back.

"You wait here in the car, Bruce. I won't be but a minute."

She was grateful he hadn't come in with her. For while Mr. Wetzel leaned his cane against the chopping block, and cut up the meat for her, his wife said, "I was just wishing one of you Belfords would come in. I have bananas to give you." She was putting a half-dozen with very black skins into a sack. "Most people think bananas have to be pale yellow. They don't know they digest better when they're soft and ripe."

It was things like this that tried Katie Rose's soul. If only her mother weren't so small-town friendly with everyone! She brought cucumbers from O'Byrne vines in Bannon to the Wetzels. They made them into dills, and sold them for ten cents each. In turn, they gave the Belfords cheese at wholesale—and overripe bananas for nothing.

Katie Rose thanked her. But she folded the top of the sack over several times and hoped, as she got into

Bruce's car, that he couldn't smell those overripe bananas.

Strange, too, how driving down Hubbell Street with Bruce, made the big old houses look more ancient and drear, and the new jerry-built ones more cheap and brazen. Their own two-story, red brick on the corner seemed shabbier, more added-onto, and spilled out of. Why did there always have to be clothes on the line? Why did their dog have to dot the lawn and porch with bones, and the littles leave their bicycles strewed about?

Each bike was fitted with a gray canvas bag for carrying papers. The littles shared an early-morning paper route. But why wasn't Mother more strict about their leaving a clutter of papers and twine on the front porch?

With Bruce stopping in front of their house and helping her out, even Cully, who rushed upon them with his overwhelming welcome, seemed more of a mongrel and in need of training.

"What kind of a dog is he?" Bruce asked.

"Just mutt," she admitted.

They were on the sidewalk and Katie Rose was still fending off Cully when someone yelled, "Hey! Hey —wait!" A girl with a reddish blond pony tail was hurrying down the street, her plaid pleated skirt swishing about her bare knees. The collar of her white blouse was half in, half out of the green blazer with the lettering SJH for St. Jude's High on the pocket. Her cheeks were rosy pink.

A basketball on top of her stack of books rolled off and bounced on the sidewalk toward Bruce. He caught it with deft ease and dribbled it on the cement. Katie Rose introduced him and her younger sister, and Stacy's bright blue eyes turned even brighter.

"You're the Bruce Seerie that never misses baskets. I wish I was half as good as you are."

A wince of pain passed over his face. "I'm off the team as of today. Old Jacoby, our lit teacher, saw to that."

Stacy, the impulsive, laid her hand on his arm. "That breaks my heart, Bruce—honest. I have a terrible time in lit too. I just finished four pages about what that poor old Ancient Marner had on his mind—"

"The Ancient *Mariner*," Katie Rose corrected and explained to Bruce, "Stacy's awful about getting words all mixed up."

Stacy, undaunted, went on, "And right now I'm reading about all the stiff-necked dodoes in '*Pride and Perjurious*' and—"

"For heaven's sake, Stacy—*Prejudice*."

"I'm not literary like Katie Rose," Stacy admitted, "but I'll give you my recipe for reading books, Bruce. I pretend that I'm the main character and that I'm right there, and I sort of think and feel like he does or she does. That's what I'm trying to do in 'Pride and Perjurious'—"

She looked at Katie Rose and laughed guiltily. Bruce laughed with her. He handed her back the basketball. "Who's your coach at St. Jude's?"

"Andy Kern. He's studying to be a priest out at the seminary, but he comes in on Mondays and Wednesdays and when we have our games Saturday afternoons. Only I wish we—or some of our neighbors—had a basket tacked up so I could practice because—"

The front door opened in the Belford house and Jill yelled, "Katie Rose, and Stacy! Ben said for you to come on in because it's almost suppertime."

"—because we've got this tough game coming up, and I need to practice free throws," Stacy finished. "*You* never miss."

"It's just practice," he said modestly, and turned toward his car.

Katie Rose couldn't bear to let him go without something definite to tie to. "If you redo your *Old Man and*— I could look it over for you tomorrow."

"Thanks, Katie Rose. I'll work on it this evening. I'm also grounded every night until I get caught up in lit." No, it wasn't like him to sound so soured on the world. "I'll bring a rewrite tomorrow, and we'll coke-up at Downey's."

Those beautiful words! "We'll coke-up at Downey's."

His cream-colored convertible was speeding down Hubbell when Katie Rose and Stacy went inside.

The downstairs of the Belford house was as unprivate as Katie Rose's own life. Anyone could stand in the reception hall and see and hear what was going on in the whole house. You couldn't see into the kitchen, but you could whiff whatever was cooking. There was no smell of cooking this early evening on the first day of March, but only a strong etherish one.

Mother sat at the table in the big room that was both living and dining room. She lifted her red head from the blue silken mass in her lap on which she was sewing, and smiled at them absently. The ether smell came from a pair of blue satin shoes which the twins waved triumphantly under Katie Rose's nose. "Look, they're dry already. Touch one and see. Go on, touch one—it isn't sticky."

Each of the girls put a testing finger on the stiff satin.

"We put two coats on," Brian said. "Fast as you put it on, it dries. We've got enough to do it again."

"Don't," Mother said, without looking up. "The

whole house smells enough like an operating room already."

Ben, the oldest of the children, came in from the kitchen. It was never Mother the young Belfords had to fear for their misdemeanors or their slipping up on some chore. It was Ben.

When the littles came home from a neighborhood battle with torn T-shirts and scattered cuts and bruises, it was he who sent them to bed without their suppers. When Katie Rose or Stacy settled themselves for a lengthy phone conversation, it was Ben who brought the timer from the kitchen and placed it beside them with the bell set to ring remindingly when five minutes were up.

"Ben, I just got started, and I still have to—"

"Anyone can say all he needs to say in five minutes."

The others accepted his bossy jurisdiction with better grace than Katie Rose. When sparks flew in the Belford house, it was between them.

This early evening he took the sack of groceries from her. "Do you by any chance think stew will cook in ten minutes?"

"Oh, for heaven's sake. I had other things to think about."

Ben had a maddening way of speaking not to her, but to an invisible someone behind her. He did now, rolling his eyes with strained patience, "Why, of course. The Duchess of Belford can't be bothered with such prosaic matters. What're a few empty stomachs to her?"

Mother bit off her sewing thread and stood up, shaking out the blue dress. "Never mind, never mind. There're always a few thises and thats we can scurry up. Maybe I'd better run the iron over the darts I took up. I didn't think it'd be much of a job, but Lord help us—all that lining and whalebone. I broke three needles. Look, Katie Rose and Stacy, feel how much heavier and richer the satin was in the old days. Wasn't that nice of Miguel's grandmother to dig through old trunks and find this for me?"

Ben was still being his sarcastic self. "If it isn't asking too much of the Duchess, I'll be needing a white jacket to wear to work tonight."

That was another chore that had slipped Katie Rose's mind when Bruce said, "How about us driving to Downey's Drug?" A clean white jacket was a must for Ben who worked evenings as sandwich man at the Ragged Robin drive-in on the Boulevard. Washing them in their old wringer-type washer was no problem. Keeping one ironed and ready for Ben each evening was.

Katie Rose ironed it in the kitchen while the family hunted up thises and thats. Tonight, it was scrambled eggs, warmed-up beans, and cabbage salad. *And* over-ripe bananas.

But the Belfords were the adaptable, easy-to-please kind. They ate with relish while everyone talked, regardless of whether anyone listened or not. Stacy was extolling Coach Kern, and worrying about their first league game this coming Saturday. The littles were telling of a new *Call* subscriber they had procured. There always seemed to be a drive for more *Call* customers. Whenever there was work for them around the house, the three said reproachfully, "But we got to go out and solicit new business."

As usual, the family lingered at the table until Ben glanced at the clock and nudged Mother, and she said, "Heavens above! It's time I was dressing for Giddy's."

She plucked her heavy silk dress off the ironing board and made for the stairs in her stocking feet. She was forever stepping out of her shoes and then forgetting where she left them.

As always, the young Belfords hovered in the hall. It was suspenseful and exciting to have Mother go scurrying up the stairs in her workaday garb, and then to descend those same stairs a beautiful and glamorous entertainer. As always Ben, his white jacket over his arm, called up to prod her. "Hurry up, gorgeous, or we'll both be late."

He drove her to Guido's Gay Nineties out on the

Henderson Road and then swung back to the Ragged Robin.

She came down the stairs this evening, all soft rustle of long and voluminous satin skirts. It was not only the blue sparkle of her eyes, or the transparent skin that often goes with red hair, but a radiant glow about her that made people turn to look at her a second time. She made no secret about her age. Everyone knew she had been twenty when Ben was born, and that he was past seventeen. But when, as now, Katie Rose saw her with her bright hair done up in a soft pompadour, and wearing the long jet earrings which matched the jet trim on the donated periwinkle— Oh, no wonder folks that gathered around the piano at Giddy's would never believe she had children in high school!

She sent the twins scampering for her newly-dyed shoes. She laughed as she slid her feet into them, "I hope Giddy's lasagne will drown out their smell."

It was an evening ritual for Brian to hold her velvet wrap for her. "My littlest own," Mother called him. She stooped low so that he could tuck it around her shoulders. Katie Rose had the last minute job of applying her lipstick; Mother never got in the corners.

With Ben hurrying her, she turned from the doorway as she always did to say, "Be good while I'm gone, and don't let the wolf in the door."

And that was the moment when Katie Rose loved her most. That was the moment when she forgave her for not following a schedule like most housewives. Imagine anyone coming home at one o'clock at night, and doing a huge washing just because she felt like it! Katie Rose forgave her for being sputtery and quick-tempered. She even forgave her for being so slapdash about her own wardrobe, and for the bargains she brought home for all of them from rummage sales and Goodwill stores. How many times had Katie Rose said, "I loathe wearing clothes someone else has worn"?

Katie Rose couldn't say why this moment put an ache in her throat. But when Mother turned at the door there was so much love for them all in her shaky smile. "Be good while I'm gone." But it was as though she said, "I wish I didn't have to leave you. I wish I could do more for all of you."

Stacy always answered, "We'll let no wolf in unless he whistles." But Katie Rose, on an impulse she couldn't resist, always reached over and kissed her mother. "Don't worry, Mom, we'll be fine till you come home."

The house always seemed empty and lonely with her going.

The next morning Katie Rose was again at the ironing board while all the breakfast hubbub went on about her. She had washed her violet ruffled blouse along with Ben's white jacket last night. She was ironing both this morning, the blouse to wear to school—surely today Bruce would notice that it gave her eyes a purplish cast—and Ben's jacket in case she and Bruce lingered long over cokes at Downey's after school.

The Belford dining room was used for everything but dining. Mother's portable sewing machine sat on one end of the table; around it the young Belfords studied, and on it the littles folded their morning papers at five A.M. The table was cleared off only for company or holiday dinners. The family breakfasted, tea-ed, and dined in what they called Mom's dinette.

It had been the back porch off the kitchen until

Mother had been inspired to rip out the wall between and turn the porch into a room with long table and benches—the handiest gathering place in the house. Mother's father, Grandda O'Byrne, was a builder in Bannon, and he had come in to aid and abet in the remodeling.

Now the family had another project: changing the closet under the stairs into half a bath. "Just that one bath upstairs, and six of us getting ready for school in the morning, is murder—plain murder," either Katie Rose or Stacy said every morning.

A sugar bowl with a broken handle held the half-a-bath fund. In it went Mother's tips from Giddy's. The morning ritual was to count the contents of the sugar bowl, add the few bills and silver Mother had brought home the night before and gloat or grieve, depending on its progress.

The up-and-down fund. The reached-into fund. There were always the unpredictables—the vet bill for Cully when a fish bone stuck in his throat; new mittens for Stacy when she lost hers in zero weather; or one of the littles saying, "Mom, Sister Ursula says tomorrow is positively the last day for us to bring our Korean orphan money."

This morning Stacy ordered, "Jill, stir the breakfast food."

"I'm counting the half-a-bath."

"Here, Matt, butter the toast while it's warm."

No answer to that, but a muffled mutter from under the table, "It was a quarter we dropped."

"I wish you'd listen," Stacy said. "They're worse than the poor old miser counting his gold in *Silas Mariner.*"

"*Marner,*" corrected Katie Rose at the ironing board.

Mother, cup in hand, waited at the stove for the coffee burbling under the percolator's glass dome to darken. The morning was chill, and she clutched a plaid robe about her and blinked her heavy eyes sleepily. Ben, both bossy and protective of her, scolded, "You were late again last night. You ought to stay in bed and get your sleep out, woman."

She murmured around a yawn, "I can always catch a nap later on."

"Seventy-seven dollars and forty cents," Matthew announced. "Where are your tips from last night, Mom?"

She said impatiently, "Who made this coffee? It certainly looks like a pale brew."

"Give it time, Mrs. Belford," Katie Rose said.

Jill demanded, "How much did you get last night, Mom, and what'd you do with it?"

Mother poured herself a cup of coffee, took a spoonful of it before she answered, "I didn't get any."

"You didn't get any! Not *any?*" came the amazed chorus from the littles. Katie Rose, too, looked up from her ironing. "But you said there was to be a big reunion party out there last night?"

Mother nodded. "There was. The tenth reunion of a college graduating class. Mostly young marrieds of course with little children at home, and some of the wives pregnant. Most of them would have to pay baby-sitters when they got home. And you know how young couples are making payments on houses and cars and TVs and washers. They were sweet. They showed me pictures of their kids. I wouldn't hear of their passing the hat for me." Her sip of coffee brought her out of her sleepy trance. She hummed "Anniversary Waltz" under her breath.

Disappointedly, the littles put the money back in the sugar bowl. Brian said, "Too bad it wasn't the Railroad Men." Their banquet would go down in Belford history; they had tipped Mother twenty dollars.

Katie Rose did the last ruffle on her blouse. "What about you, Mom? Did you make a big hit in your beaded periwinkle satin and matching slippers?"

Mother's young giggle spilled over. She said, "I want the whole caboodle of you congregated here between seven and seven-thirty this evening."

Stacy gave a gleeful shriek. "The Ardor Dampeners, huh?"

Mother's piano playing and singing, her bubbling laugh, her friendly warmth often attracted a gentleman diner at Giddy's. Usually, the enamoured one inquired of Guido and found that she was a widow. Usually, he didn't believe her when she said she had six children at home, but thought it was her way of putting him off.

Ben looked up with his watchdog alertness. "Who is he?"

She stifled another yawn. "Robert something—it's a real nice-sounding last name. He gave me his card only I don't know what I did with it. But he insisted on calling for me to take me to work tonight."

Brian, the worrier, said, "You aren't going to marry him, are you, Mom?"

She reached over and brushed his cheek. "No, my littlest dear, don't worry. He won't get within shootin' distance after tonight."

Mother was on her second cup of coffee and her first cigarette when the six Belfords snatched up their books and their six sacks of lunch. They loaded themselves in their noisy Chevvie with Ben at the wheel. He dropped the three littles and Stacy at the old red brick St. Jude's, and then swung east toward John Quincy Adams High.

On other mornings, Katie Rose would have said, "Let me drive the rest of the way." Now that she was past sixteen, Mother said that Ben should teach her to drive. But Ben was neither a patient teacher, nor Katie Rose a docile student.

This morning she didn't mention driving. She had other things on her mind. She had a feeling that Jeanie might not appreciate this new and wonderful alliance between an A student in lit and an F one. But any uneasiness was crowded out by a quivery looking forward to sitting across the table from Bruce at Downey's this afternoon.

She hadn't told Jeanie yet when, after French II, Katie Rose, Jeanie, and Miguel were swept along in the rush to the lunchroom and "lunch with the bunch." Because they brought their lunches, they always had a few minutes alone at the table for eight while the other five waited in line at the lunch counter.

Miguel asked, "Petunia, are you trying out after school with Mrs. Dujardin?"

"No, she's out of school today. I was told it's a virus."

"Then how about another driving lesson?"

She gave him a flustered look. "Not today, Miguel, because I'm going—I mean I just happen to have something else after school."

Jeanie looked curious, and Miguel asked, "Like what?"

She was saved an answer by the appearance of two boys with hot-dog sandwiches and pink ice cream. Both boys had ginger-colored hair, horn-rimmed glasses; both wore snug Levis, and checked shirts. They shared a passionate interest in stripped-down stock cars, and ownership in one they lovingly referred to as Decrepit Old Delia. Madame in French II, unable to distinguish which was John and which Tom, called them both John-Tom.

George, a very polite boy from the Philippines, quietly slid into his chair.

Next came June bearing a tray with a plate lunch, chocolate milk, and a piece of cocoanut pie. It always amazed Katie Rose that anyone so frail and flowerlike could do so well by food. George leaped to help her unload her tray. June rewarded him with her little Mona Lisa smile.

"Make way for the small tornado," muttered one of the John-Toms.

The small tornado was Deetsy, delayed by talking to her latest crush who happened to be Howard, the drama teacher's right hand. Deetsy came to the table with only a glass of orange juice and a bowl of cottage cheese; this was one of her dieting periods. She dropped her change as she sat down, and again George leaped up to retrieve some pennies and a nickel off the floor.

"I looked for a quarter to put my foot on," Miguel said with his urchin grin.

Deetsy shook out her paper napkin—somewhat dampened by orange juice—and blurted out, "Hey, did you hear Bruce Seerie got kicked off the team because Jacoby failed him? And I hear that you, Katie Rose, are going into a huddle with him every afternoon at Downey's Drug. Howie told me."

Old Walkie-talkie Deetsy. The boy behind the fountain must have told Howard and he had told Deetsy—and Deetsy was telling the world.

June, who was the most untalkative at the table except George, suddenly giggled. "You've taken on a lot, Katie Rose. I remember when we were in junior high and we had one of those quizzes where you match up authors with titles. Bruce put Milton with *The Village Blacksmith,* and Shakespeare with *Huckleberry Finn.*"

One of the John-Toms asked with owlish innocence, "Who did write *Huck Finn?* Hawthorne?"

Katie Rose avoided looking at Jeanie or Miguel. She said, "Bruce—well, he has to do over his report on *The Old Man and*—and so I—"

"And the story of his life," Miguel put in. "Jacoby will never let him throw a basketball until he does. And no skimpy little two or three pages either. He wants an opus of ten or twelve—"

"That's enough literary conversation," either John or Tom said, much to Katie Rose's relief. "Who's got a leftover can of paint to donate for another stripe or square on Delia? We're giving her a coat of many colors like Jacob's in the Bible—or was it Jacob?"

"Joseph," Miguel said.

Katie Rose said instantly, "I'll hunt up a can or two for you. Mom always has paint left over from this or that job."

"A few more daubs and old Delia will be ready to roll. We can't decide which of you pretties will be the first one to ride in her." Their two pairs of eyes, bright as a terrier's, roamed over the four girls at the table. "Not you, Jeanie, though your light poundage is in your favor, but your old man would be afraid for you to set forth in a car that's weathered thirty-two winters."

"How right you are," Jeanie said ruefully.

"And not you, June. You're too well surrounded by Adams's hearty athletes."

"How about me?" Deetsy asked. "I'm losing weight every day."

"No, not you. You're too busy haunting poor old Howard in the greenroom off the stage." Their twin gaze rested on Katie Rose. "But you, with the purple eyes, if you sit light and pray hard, we'll give you the first ride in Delia in her new coat of many colors."

"Hey, Petunia's my girl, remember?" Miguel said. "If you take her, you'll have to take me too."

"If we have to, we have to," they agreed.

Katie Rose laughed. Yes, in a way she was Miguel's girl. He was like family in the Belford house. He often brought Stacy home from basketball practice in his old and battered Mercedes. He was as concerned as the Belfords themselves about the half-a-bath fund which had been going up and down for two years.

The bell rang.

In the short interim between lunch and study hour when Katie Rose and Jeanie were at their locker, Katie Rose said, "I was going to tell you about Bruce —I mean my helping him—when you phoned last night, but Stacy and the littles were racketing around—"

"It isn't a state secret, is it?"

"Of course not. You see, Jeanie, I was standing right here at the locker when all of them—Coach, Jacoby, Mr. Knight, and Bruce, and his mother— came out of the office. Honest, you never saw anyone look so—so sort of whipped and lost as Bruce. And Mrs. Seerie looking so Mother-knows-best—"

"I know, I know. But I remember nursing you through times when you were pretty whipped and lost yourself."

"Oh come now, you don't have to make such a

thing out of it. I'm just going to help him so he—"

"Are you sure you won't start worshiping again, Katie Rose? I hate to see you take him out of the storeroom. You aren't *right* for Bruce. I wasn't either."

Katie Rose gave a tinny laugh. "Have you decided just who is this *right* girl for Bruce?"

"Don't get lofty." They walked on to study hall. At the door Jeanie stopped to say musingly, "Bruce is parent-ridden. I don't mean they're monsters, but all his life they've molded him into their idea of the clean-cut American boy—the nice, well-mannered, well-muscled athlete. And gosh, Katie Rose, Bruce isn't *right* for you. You're yourself with Miguel and the lunch bunch. But you're not with Bruce. You're so busy trying to make him think you're wonderful—why, I wouldn't know."

Katie Rose would have resented such candor from anyone else, but not Jeanie when her face was crinkled in concern. Katie Rose said haltingly, "It isn't because Bruce lives in such a swanky house, or drives a yummy car—"

"Half his, and half his mother's," Jeanie corrected shortly. "And Bruce knows if he doesn't toe the mark he'll be afoot."

Miguel joined them as they walked inside. He was

gulping and swallowing. "There, I got the last of that dratted apple down." The three paused briefly at their seats. "No sun today to brighten our lives," he commented, and then abruptly, "Petunia, I'm beginning to seethe. Here I wangle Grandpop's Dodge to give you a driving lesson after school, and you give me a vague runaround about being busy, and then Deetsy—"

"Oh, that Deetsy!" Katie Rose glanced at Jeanie, hoping she'd say as she did so often, "You can discount ninety percent of what Deetsy says." But Jeanie said nothing.

Katie Rose stammered, "Bruce is in an awful hole —and so I promised I'd read a book report—he was going to do it over last night." She looked at her two best friends and added defiantly, "I don't see why everyone's getting so steamed up about my helping Bruce get a passing mark in lit so Coach can put him back on the team. Everyone says we won't have a chance at the championship without his shooting baskets."

"I weep for the team," said Jeanie.

"My school spirit will just stretch so far," said Miguel as he shambled himself into his seat. But he gave Katie Rose his warm, ragamuffin grin, "I like to be appreciated."

Katie Rose glanced at Bruce as he sat across the booth from her in Downey's Drug. She didn't know what to say to him about his rewritten book report on *The Old Man and the Sea.*

She shuffled his three scant pages together. He had failed to find any symbolic meaning. To him it was only the story of an old man catching a huge marlin which the sharks gnawed completely away before he finally reached shore. Where Bruce used his own phrasing and not Hemingway's, it was wooden and trite.

"Bruce, weren't you moved—I mean didn't you feel sorry for the poor old fellow having to eat raw fish to keep up his strength? Didn't you just ache over his sore hands?"

He shook his head emphatically. "No, not a bit. Because if he'd had any sense he'd have let the fish go, and streaked on back to shore. I would have."

"But, you see, catching that fish stood for—"

Again they were interrupted. The Unprivate Life of Katie Rose! This time it was Miguel. Now why had he come? He didn't look "seething." He looked his usual friendly, impudent self.

"Hi, Petunia. Hi, Bruce. I thought maybe I'd find you here. How're you coming on prose and poetry, Bruce?"

"Neither fast nor furious. I've got an oral on *Hamlet* left over from last semester. Then that autobiography Jacoby is making such a stew about. At least ten pages, he said. I could write the story of my life in one."

Miguel stepped to the fountain for a bottle of coke, and pushed in beside Katie Rose. "I like Jacoby's idea of not having it just 'I was born on such and such a date, and when I was five I spent the summer with Aunt Hortense.' He was telling our class how our dark days and our bright are often mileposts in our lives, and he wants to hear about them." He flashed them a sidewise smile. "So I gave him two pages of my fighting a kid named Micky Dunn."

Bruce said with a faint edge of superiority, "Fighting with your fists never solves a thing. Dad dinged that into me from the time I got my first tricycle."

But the Irish side of Katie Rose prompted her, "What did you fight about, Miguel, and who won?"

"It wasn't a case of fighting *about* anything. It was when Dad was getting material for his book on Ireland and I was boarded out near Cork. I was such a piddlin', scared little rabbit of a kid, and every morning of the world when I set out to school this Micky Dunn laid for me at the corner behind a blackberry hedge. I always got the worst of it. So one drizzly morning when I was dreading to set forth, I happened to see a big black rosary somebody had left laying on the table. Its beads were the size of beans, and it had a heavy cross at the end. It looked to me like the only salvation at hand, and so I snitched it—"

Katie Rose gave an appreciative titter. "That's why Ben won't let our littles carry rosaries—they're apt to use them for weapons too."

Miguel went on, "And the minute Micky leaped out at me, I whipped that rosary sixty ways for Sunday all over his face and neck. It blinded him. To this day I bet he doesn't know what hit him, and to this day I wonder I didn't put out an eye. But that was the first morning I ever went to school unbludgeoned and unbruised."

Katie Rose laughed joyfully. Bruce said with even greater emphasis, "My dad's a lawyer. He always says lawyers make a lot of their dough just on people that lose their heads and start fighting it out."

Katie Rose stirred uneasily. "But you take boxing, Bruce. You even won an award in the All-City—"

"Sure, but that was skill. I like sports that take skill and endurance like football and apparatus gym and skiing and—" he winced as he added, "basketball."

Miguel drained his coke bottle. "But haven't you ever been so mad you didn't care whether you had your head pounded in or not, just so you could get some good licks in?"

Bitterness settled again on Bruce's chiseled features. "Right now I'm so mad at Jacoby that even the thought of him turns my stomach. Okay, so where would it get me to take a swat at him?"

"In the hoosegow, no doubt," Miguel grinned. "Petunia, I almost forgot what I came for. Your mother wants you to come home. She's got a grand surprise for you, and she needs your help besides."

"A surprise? You don't mean the folks from Bannon?" That would be no grand surprise. Mother's relatives and old friends were always driving that fifty-seven miles between Denver and Bannon. The surprise was that Mother could always find room to put them up.

"A grander surprise than that," Miguel said knowingly.

So the Aid-for-Bruce session ended with his driving home alone, while Miguel took Katie Rose to Hubbell Street in his low and rattly beetle of a car and had to help her out over the door on her side which wouldn't open.

Grandda O'Byrne's pickup with its mud-splashed Bannon license was parked at the curb.

She and Miguel went through the picket gate at the side and through the back door into the dining room, and took the few steps into the front hall. And into pandemonium, clutter, and wild excitement. One of the littles shrieked the glad tidings first, "Katie Rose, we're going to get our half-a-bath. And whatta you know! —a shower too."

Mother, flushed and beaming, turned and threw her arms around both Miguel and Katie Rose. "Yes, would you believe it?—Leo and Grandda say we can squeeze in a shower. By knocking out that kitchen wall where the cupboard is—the pot and pan cupboard—but we can do with less cupboard space. And look, Miguel—look, Katie Rose! Aren't they beautiful?"

"They've been used," Jill put in, "but Grandda got them out of a house where they didn't want them. For just a song."

"They" were a small corner washbowl and toilet, sitting naked and unabashed in a corner of the hall, the washbowl tilted against the piano. This thought brushed the edge of Katie Rose's mind: Wasn't it a blessing that it was Miguel and not Bruce who had come in with her?

She gathered, from all the talk, that Grandda had remodeled a house in Bannon, and the owners had said he could have the old bathroom fixtures for whatever he wanted to pay. He had remembered the Belfords in Denver and their longing for a downstairs bath. He had sought out the Callanan boys who were plumbers, and "loose connections" of the family—meaning that they, too, had come from Cork County in Ireland. Leo Callanan said it was a slack time in the plumbing business and sure, he'd come in and see about putting in that half-a-bath for Rose. And then to find he could squeeze in a shower as well!

"What about the dough?" Miguel asked. "Have you got enough in the up-and-down fund?"

"Leo said he'd take what we had, and then I can pay the balance as I get it," Mother answered.

Grandda backed out of the closet. He was winding up his round metal tapeline, and he gave Katie Rose his roguish O'Byrne smile and wink. "What about you, little blackbird? Would you rather have a shower and less cupboard space?"

"Oh yes. A shower will be heaven."

But who'd ever think a wrap closet under the stairs

could hold so much? Katie Rose looked appalled at the piles of apparel that had been tossed onto the piano and bench, the dining table—even the stairs. And such a scattering of old schoolbooks, broken cameras, lost mittens. As she stepped over to deposit her books on the stairs, her foot struck an old quart can of paint. It was red, and there was enough in it to shake. She could donate that to the John-Toms and their repainting decrepit Delia.

The littles were having a field day. So was Miguel. He had already picked up a handful of marbles, and he and Matt were admiring a smoky and a bull's-eye. Jill stood holding a long-handled, wire corn-popper, fascinated by the cover that slid off and then back, and fastened with a clip at the end. "I didn't know we had this. Miguel, what's it got such a long handle for?"

"That's so you can pop corn over a fireplace without burning your hand."

An enrapt Brian was holding what looked like a small clipboard. "I had this when I was a little child," he said. "And then it disappeared and I forgot all about it. See, Miguel and Katie Rose, it's a magic slate. Only it's not really a slate but this waxy white paper. And you use this little pencil—only it's not really a pencil but sharpened like a pencil—to write on it. Go ahead, Miguel, and write something on it."

Miguel took the small pencil that wasn't a pencil and wrote, "Petunia is a dope."

Brian lifted the top white sheet off its black under-layer, and the words disappeared. "You see, it's magical," he said happily.

Katie Rose laughed. "I'm not a dope now. Hurray!"

Ben and Leo came up from the basement where Leo was investigating "lead-off" pipes. He was a short, slightly balding man with a ruddy complexion. "Looks okay so far. But you never know what you're going to run into."

Ben's interest, too, was caught by one of the items that came from the catch-all under the stairs. A pair of red earmuffs. He dusted them off with his sleeve. He met Katie Rose's eye and said a little sheepishly, "You know how Jeanie's always having trouble with her ears? I told her once she ought to wear earmuffs when it's cold and blowy, and she said you couldn't buy them any more. These are sort of antiques—but why don't you ask her—"

"Ask her yourself, Ben. She'd look cute in red ear-muffs." There were rare moments when she felt close and loving to Ben . . . . "He's so doggoned bossy," she complained often to Jeanie.

"I like bossy men," Jeanie always said.

Stacy came in from school and was told the glad

news by everyone. "A shower!" she rejoiced. "A rooty-tooty shower! Oh, Leo, I'll love you forever," and she threw her arms around him.

Grandda was still jotting down measurements, and talking plumbing to Mother and Leo. At times like these when he was all builder, it was hard for Katie Rose to realize that in his early days he had been one of the Abbey players in Dublin. He still acted in and directed plays in the Bannon territory.

Even now his big frame had no stoop. His eyes were surprisingly blue and bright in his weathered face under shaggy, bleached-out eyebrows. He was very proud of the fact that his great thatch of red hair had no sprinkling of gray in it.

Again his roguish eyes lit on Katie Rose. "I thought sure a man would be offered a cup of tea in this house before he took a long drive home."

"Land of love, what are we thinking of!" Mother exclaimed. "Katie Rose, go put on the kettle. And see if there's enough water on the stew while you're there."

After tea, Miguel departed for his grandparents' six blocks to the south, and Grandda for Bannon fifty-seven miles to the north.

Later on Leo, who would stay until the weekend, was crowded in at the long table in the dinette. They all ate the Mulligan stew that Mother had planned for

the night before. Leo and Mother talked about speci-
fications demanded by the plumbing code until Ben
nudged her and pointed to the clock. "God help us,"
she murmured, "it's time I was dressing for Giddy's."

In all the excitement and hubbub no one remembered—not even Mother—that she was to be called
for by an admirer named Robert with a very nice-
sounding last name she couldn't remember.

The doorknocker sounded long before Mother de-
scended the stairs. Katie Rose was sweeping up some
of the debris of checkers and monopoly games. She
leaned her broom against the newel post and opened
the door on what the O'Byrnes would call "a fine figure of a man." He was wearing a tweed topcoat, and
he handed her a box wrapped in white paper and said
genially, "I thought you children might like some
candy. Your mother is expecting me. I'm Bob Rotharmel."

"Oh yes—yes. Thank you for the candy. Come in,
Mr. Rotharmel." (It certainly *was* a nice-sounding
name.)

He stepped inside. The look of startled disbelief on
his face grew. And no wonder, Katie Rose thought.
His foot hit a ping-pong ball and sent it clattering
across the floor. And why hadn't someone thought to
throw a covering over the detached washbowl and
toilet there at the end of the piano? Stacy had found

one roller skate, and she came skating into the hall saying, "I wish I could find the other one."

Katie Rose introduced Stacy and Mr. Rotharmel.

Ben came in from the kitchen with his white jacket over his arm, all ready to call up the stairs, "Hurry up, gorgeous, or you'll be late."

He stopped short at sight of the visitor. Katie Rose fumbled through an introduction to Ben.

They were shaking hands when the littles came rushing out of the living room bearing the long-handled popcorn popper which gave out an acrid cloud of smoke. "It popped so pretty and then it turned black. What made it burn?"

Ben turned into his scolding self. "Who told you kids you could build a fire in the fireplace? Don't you know better than to pop corn over a roaring fire? You're supposed to wait till it burns down to coals or embers. Now don't go wasting butter on that burnt mess, d'you hear?"

With that, Mother came tripping down the stairs. Tonight she was wearing her emerald green taffeta with its black lace yoke, and black lace cuffs that came up to the elbow in the leg-of-mutton sleeves. She had a moment of bewildered surprise that gave her pause on the middle step. She surveyed the nice-looking but dismayed man surrounded by the popcorn poppers, Stacy hobbling on one skate, and Ben and Katie Rose.

But on the bottom step she laughed and held out her hand to him. "It isn't always quite this wild and woolly around here, Mr.—Mr.—"

"Just settle for Bob," he said.

"But today is a most unusual day. We're getting ready for half-a-bath in the hall closet here."

"Oh," he said, but he still looked dismayed.

Little Brian touched his mother's arm. "We were hurrying to make popcorn in the popper we found so you could take some with you and eat it while you played the piano. But it burned and burned."

"We just shook it and shook it," Jill said, and her twin added, "We shook the very bejabers out of it."

Mother said, "Katie Rose, you help them make some more when their fire dies down. Oh, for mercy's sake, who did what with my cape that was hanging in the closet?"

It was found buried in the pile of wraps draped over the piano. Mr. Rotharmel, dazed as he was, reached for it to hold for her.

"Brian always does that," Jill reproved.

Brian held the cape for her. Katie Rose applied her lipstick. Stacy skated through the house on her one skate until she found Mother's black lace mitts.

She and Mr. Rotharmel went out the door together. The young Belfords waited until they heard the slam of his car door, and then Ben threw back his head and laughed his hearty, infectious guffaw. "Well, if it was Ardor Dampeners she wanted, she sure got them in full force tonight."

Stacy was unwrapping the box of candy. "We'll never see him around these parts again. He's nice too. And lookit!—it says right on the box 'Net weight three pounds.' "

Brian was the first to ask Mother the next morning, "Is the man who brought the candy last night coming for you again?"

She was standing in the doorway of the empty closet talking to Leo, and she answered absently, "I doubt it."

"What does he do?" Ben wanted to know.

"The corner washbowl will come to about here, Leo. Gosh, Ben, I can't remember what he said he did. I can't even remember his name."

"Rotharmel," Stacy said. "I remember because it rhymes with carmel, and there were carmels in the candy he—"

"Car-a-mels," Katie Rose corrected.

Jill grumbled, "Yeh, and Stacy stuck her thumb nail in all the pieces to see which were caramels."

Mother's temper flared. "Stacy! I've told you and told you—"

Stacy backed swiftly out of striking distance. "Just a few, Mom, honest. And I barely gave them a little teensy poke on the underneath side to see if they were hard. Katie Rose, why don't you give Mom and Leo a cup of coffee?"

Everyone laughed at that, even Mother and Leo. Everyone knew Stacy's reasoning: Mother was never so apt to swat an offender if she had a cup of coffee in her hand.

The ground was covered with a fine sleet when Mother held open the back door for the hurried exodus of the six pupils out of the house and into the car. She stopped Katie Rose to say, "Lovey, couldn't you go over to see Grandfather Belford after school this afternoon?"

"After school? Why?"

Of course Mother couldn't know that those after-school hours were now dedicated and sacred. Not that anyone else considered them sacred either. The littles had interrupted her Aid-to-Bruce on Monday with their frantic reminders of the meat for Mulligan stew. Miguel had interrupted yesterday because of the Grand Surprise for her at home.

Mother went on, "I worry about him there alone with Aunt Eustace away at Palm Springs. He's been

indoors with a cold—not sick enough to be in bed—
and it'd be nice if you called on him. It's pretty lonely
for him in that huge old mausoleum by himself."

"He's got Mrs. Van."

"Oh, but a housekeeper isn't family. I'd go myself
only I want to help Leo. Grandfather would be tickled to death if you'd get to the Belford mansion in
time to have tea with him."

Katie Rose was wondering what excuse she could
think up, when a thought struck her: Why couldn't
she ask Bruce to go to the Belford mansion with her?
Understanding poetry was part of his getting a passing mark from Jacoby. And no one knew poetry better than Grandfather Belford—Chancellor Belford,
he was.

There was another reason which Katie Rose
couldn't quite put into words. She might feel apologetic about this corner brick house as compared to the
Seeries' modern, split-level one—and those three
baths, when the Belfords' second was a major event in
their lives. But a girl need feel not the slightest apology about the elegance of the Belford mansion.

"Okay, Mom, I'll go."

"Tell him we're getting our downstairs bath,"
Mother said just as Ben called out, "All aboard!"

She saw Bruce at the drinking fountain when she
left math. She invited him to go with her to Grandfa-

ther Belford's after school, and he said yes, he'd be glad to. He was not only polite, but *docile* as though life had few choices for him these days.

It wasn't until she started for French fourth hour that she wondered about Miguel. Was he planning on a driving lesson today? Would she dare tell him she was exposing Bruce to all her grandfather's knowledge of poetry?

Miguel was not in class. He didn't appear until study hall, and then he looked rushed and worried. His grandfather, he told her and Jeanie, had fallen on a sleety step that morning when he went out for the paper. His leg had twisted under him, so that he'd had to hobble in. And what a time he and his grandmother had with the stubborn old codger to get him to a doctor for an X-ray.

"But I drove him down," Miguel said, "and, sure enough, he came home with a cast on from his shin to above the knee. I'll have to cancel our driving lesson, Petunia, so as to help Gran when I get home."

"Oh, Miguel, that's too bad," Katie Rose said, feeling a little like Judas. It wasn't that she was glad about his grandfather's accident; it was just that it saved her saying, "I've got something else after school today," and hearing his, "Like what?" or "I'm beginning to seethe."

That afternoon Bruce Seerie stopped the cream-colored convertible and helped Katie Rose out in front of the huge, gray stone house with its rounded turrets. (Silos, Ben called them.) No matter how many times she visited here, she was always struck anew by the very grandness and elegance of the place.

Bruce opened the heavy, blackish iron gates. He knew all about the Belford mansion and its occupants, because his father was Aunt Eustace's lawyer, and the families entertained back and forth. They followed the winding walk past a lily pool, and the bronze deer which a snarling wolf was trying to down.

This afternoon Katie Rose felt an extra excitement to be ringing the bell at the heavy carved door with Bruce beside her.

Grandfather Belford welcomed them both warmly. Even Mrs. Van (her real name was Vanderburg) seemed pleased to have company to tea. She brought it in promptly, complete with tiny sandwiches and *petits fours.* Would Bruce rather have a soft drink, Grandfather asked, and he said no, tea was all right.

Katie Rose's two grandfathers were the antithesis of each other. Here was Grandfather Belford in a white shirt and dark gray suit; she could remember seeing Grandda O'Byrne only once in a dark suit, and that was when he came in to her father's funeral. Grandfather's skin was like tissue paper that has been crumpled up and then smoothed out, and his hair like white silken floss; whereas Grandda's ruddy, outdoor skin was topped by that thatch of thick red hair.

Yet the two men had great respect and liking for each other. When they visited together, it surprised Katie Rose to realize how much Grandfather Belford knew about building, and how eloquently Grandda O'Byrne could talk about playwrights and poets.

Grandfather had evidently heard of Bruce's failing in lit from his parents. He asked with kindly interest, "What seems to be the biggest hurdle, Bruce?"

"I guess I'm just stupid, sir."

Katie Rose said, "Mr. Jacoby is going to give him an oral on poetry. Tell him about it, Bruce."

"It's kind of on poetry appreciation. Three of us are to take it together. Each one is supposed to sound off for about twenty minutes. We're supposed to tell him what our definition of poetry is—"

At that Grandfather quickened, a bright gleam in his eyes. His voice turned slightly oratorical. "Many people have defined poetry in many different ways. Poetry is architecture. Poetry is the language of the gods. A Frenchman said it was truth in its Sunday clothes. St. Augustine said it was devil's wine. Would you agree with any of those definitions?"

"No, sir," Bruce said frankly. "I'd say it's just a lot of words thrown together that don't make sense. Language of the gods! If they can understand it, they're smarter than I am." His bitterness was showing again.

Grandfather fitted the tips of his fingers together and studied them. He said thoughtfully, "It often helps to understand something of the man behind his poetry. Walt Whitman said,

'Camerado, this is no book,

Who touches this touches a man. . . .'

Let's compare Whitman with a man like Heinrich Heine, who was an undersized, sickly, unhappy Jew—"

Katie Rose put in, "I've read his biography. I felt so bad when he sent his first book of poems to Goethe— he looked up to him so—and Goethe never thanked him or even acknowledged it." She was a little proud of being able to show off her knowledge to Bruce.

Grandfather nodded. "Yes, poor Heine was rejected, rebuffed on all sides. So that his humor is what you might call *gallows humor*. He would laugh his high-pitched laugh to hide tears. It isn't surprising that he would write,

'Madam Sorrow . . . shows no eagerness
for flitting;
But with a long and fervent kiss
Sits by your bed—and brings her knitting.' "

Katie Rose glanced at Bruce to see if he were stirred
by this talk of the German poet. He was staring
moodily into his tea cup.

Grandfather went on, "Let's go back to Walt
Whitman. He was one of our vigorous, unconven-
tional poets. At first his work wasn't accepted—it was
even abused by critics who said he was raw and crude.
And so he was in spots, and sublime in others. But he
was not the kind of man who would *let* Madam Sorrow sit by his bed and bring her knitting. He thun-
dered out,

'Henceforth I ask not good-fortune, I
myself am good-fortune,
Henceforth I whimper no more, postpone
no more.' "

Goodness, maybe it wasn't such a good idea after all
for Katie Rose to get him launched. Chancellor Belford had given so many lectures on poetry and poets.
And he *had* been confined to the house, and he did
seem carried away by the sound of his own voice.

Yes, poets were historians, he said. Take Shakespeare. Even though he was often inaccurate with

dates and places, still young people could learn of England's descent of kings from him.

Bruce managed to say, "Yes, sir," and "No, sir," in the right places. They stood up and said their good-bys when Mrs. Van came in to clear the tea things away.

As they went back through the iron gates, Katie Rose said, "I thought maybe you'd get a sort of feel for poetry, if you heard Grandfather holding forth about it."

He said gloomily, "I got the feel of being an ignorant slob."

He stopped in front of her house. "Has Stacy been working on her free throws?" he asked.

"I haven't heard her say. They're practicing this afternoon for their game Saturday. They're playing St. Xavier's."

She didn't ask him in, for she could imagine the clutter and dishabille of the whole lower floor.

It was even worse than she imagined. Plaster dust crunched under her feet. Scrap lumber was pushed into corners. What had once been the kitchen cupboard on the other side of the stair closet was now only a yawning gap in the wall. Utensils and packaged goods were piled in cartons and on the drainboards.

Ben and Leo were leaving in the car for a plumbing supply house. Mother was slumped at the dinette table cluttered with tea things. Her red hair was mussed, and the sleeve of her blouse looked as though a nail had torn it.

Her voice was weary and driven. "Katie Rose, if you can find the aspirin, I'd better take one for my head. I'm so tired I could stretch right out here on this dinette bench and go to sleep with my head on this pile of egg beaters and pie pans. I wish it were Friday or Sunday night, so I wouldn't have to dress and go to Giddy's after supper. Supper! And I haven't an idea in the world what to have."

"We can send the littles to Wetzel's for something."

"The littles! You might know they'd disappear as soon as they slopped down their tea. Look in that carton with the shoe polish on top—I think the aspirin is there."

Katie Rose found the bottle, proffered her mother one of the white tablets. She took it with a swallow of tea. "Thuh-h, dishwater warm!"

Katie Rose laughed at her grimace. "Sit still, Mom, and I'll make you some hot. I'll bet you didn't rest any today."

"No, I was helping Leo. And I put in a call for Grandda about what lumber we'll need. And then if I didn't forget to tell him about the old-fashioned quarter round that's going to be hard to match. Oh, love, pour me a half-cup of hot tea even if it's still weak."

She stirred sugar and milk into it, took a sip. "What did Grandfather Belford say when you told him we're getting a downstairs bath?"

"If I didn't forget to tell him!" she said, and they both laughed. "I took Bruce Seerie with me. He got kicked off the basketball team because he's failing in lit, and I thought maybe Grandfather could—well, maybe inspire him on poetry."

"Heaven help us, I hope he didn't get off on Hoccleve and Chaucer. They've never yet inspired my soul."

"No, Walt Whitman and Heinrich Heine—comparisons of."

Mother said, "I'll take Yeats, with a little Ben Jonson thrown in."

"I like Emily Dickinson. Remember how Dad used to say that poets were able to say what was in the hearts of others who weren't able to say it for themselves? It's just as though she wrote one or two poems for me."

"Did she, darling? Your Emily D wrote one for me too."

Katie Rose looked at her in surprise. She had

thought that she, Katie Rose, was the poetry apprecia-
tor in the family. "She did? Which one?"

"I can't remember the words exactly. But it starts,
'You left me, sweet, two legacies. A legacy of love—'
And the other was a legacy—of—pain—" Mother's
voice broke. She cupped her face in her two hands
and there, in all the clutter of the dinette table, cried
wearily.

Katie Rose's own throat tightened. Two legacies.
The legacy of love had started in the library at the
university when a freshman from Bannon, named
Rose O'Byrne, had gone for research material and met
a young man who was working on his Master's. The
legacy of pain had started on a snowy night when the
road patrol telephoned from a little mountain town to
say a car had overturned on an icy road and a man,
identified as Benjamin Belford, had been killed.

"Don't cry, Mom—don't cry."

Mother, her face still hidden in her hands, gulped
out, "Don't mind me, lovey—it's just that I'm so tired
and discouraged—all the old pipes lay wrong for con-
necting—and a two-by-four dropped on my foot.
Then the city plumbing inspector came snooping
around—one of these too-big-for-his-britches kind—
and he and Leo had a set-to. And I feel gritty all
over."

"You go right upstairs and take a bath and lie

down," Katie Rose ordered. "It's five now, and you stay there till seven. I'll run those littles to earth, and send them to Wetzel's. I'll even bring your supper up to you."

"You're a rock of Gibraltar," her mother said gratefully.

Katie Rose listened to her faltering steps going up the stairs. I'm not a rock of Gibraltar very often, she thought guiltily.

6

Saturday was a very special day for Katie Rose. Bruce was coming this afternoon to watch *Hamlet* on TV with her. Mr. Jacoby had enjoined his classes not to miss it. His face lighted. "As you watch, notice how the action is carried on by Hamlet's confiding to the audience."

Bruce's face had not lighted at mention of his viewing *Hamlet* with her. But he, thanked her, accepted, and said he would bring cokes.

Bruce was coming! Yes, a most unusual day.

The Belford house was the kind that always had to be cleaned before company came. And this morning it was more of a Herculean task than ever because of the downstairs bath in the making. The work was at a hiatus over the weekend with Leo gone back to Bannon.

Katie Rose cornered the littles. "We've got to get all these odds and ends on the dining table put away. I want you to carry some of it upstairs, and some down to the basement."

They turned aghast faces on her. "Katie Rose, do you know what day today is?"

"Of course I know. It's Saturday, the sixth of March."

It was the first Saturday of the month, they corrected her, and the day they had to finish their collecting from the paper customers, and turn the money in.

"Or else we'll get put off the P.P.C. list," Brian added gravely.

For newspaper carriers, as Katie Rose knew, the P.P.C. was equivalent to the Purple Heart; it meant Prompt-Paying Carriers. So Katie Rose made countless trips upstairs and to the basement herself, before she was rewarded by a glimpse of the top of the dining table.

. . . The first day Bruce Seerie had walked into the life of Katie Rose Belford, they had sat at this table and drunk iced tea. Every detail of that hot Labor Day was still etched on her mind. She had cleaned the house, and put on her coral-colored dress in expectation of Grandfather Belford and Aunt Eustace. They hadn't come, and she was feeling lonely and forsaken by the world when Cully's bark announced someone at the front door. She had opened it to see a broad-shouldered boy, with a mat of black curly hair and a beautiful smile, bathed in the sunset's rosy glow. Her heart had instantly decided, "I want to be his girl." . . .

"Ben, we've got to get these awful bathroom fixtures out of the hall. Help me move them into the bathroom."

"They'll just have to be moved out again. Leo isn't ready for them yet."

"But we can't have them sitting right out here in the hall. Bruce Seerie is coming and—"

"Oh, for lord's sakes! Bruce has seen a washbowl and toilet before."

But Ben gave his whole strength to picking up first one and then the other, and sliding them into the space under the stairs. "Handle with care our precious jewels," Mother warned. Ben pretended he was dropping the washbowl just to hear her gasp.

Then there were cookies to make so Bruce could reach for one along with drinking cokes and watching *Hamlet*.

"I'll help," Stacy offered. "Let's double the recipe because I promised to bring two dozen for our Hospitality Hour after the game this aft. How about sour cream drop cookies to use the sour cream Grandda brought in?"

This was another thing that tried Katie Rose's soul. She envied the ones who had rolls of ready-to-bake cookies in their refrigerators. But Ben, the watchdog of finances, wouldn't hear to that. "You pay too much for what you get, and besides we've got butter, eggs, and such from Bannon."

She also envied the ones who could pick out a recipe and follow it. But recipes were apt to call for butter in cubes, and their butter came from Bannon in bowls or buckets. Their eggs were apt to be cracked in transit, so that the baker had to decide how many leaky eggs to use when the recipe called for three un-leaky ones. And cream! The Bannon cream was too thick to pour. Ah, the drop cookies that had run all over the pan because of their richness!

This morning the cooky making was more nerve-wracking than usual since the utensil cupboard had been demolished. Each mixing bowl and baking sheet had to be hunted for. (The egg beater was finally found under the dinette table.)

Katie Rose slid in the first panful. Ben was talking on the telephone in the hall, and she said to Stacy, "That's his lab partner he's been talking to all this time. Grace, her name is. Can you imagine a fellow talking to a girl that long about the thoraxes and tympanums of a grasshopper?"

Stacy's eyes danced. "We'll fix him." She took the timer off the shelf over the stove, set it for five minutes, and placed it on the newel post, even as Ben had done so often with her and Katie Rose.

And Katie Rose imitated Ben's gruff voice, "No sense in having a phone tied up with senseless talk while an important call gets a busy signal."

Ben had the grace to look foolish. "Never mind, never mind, you Wisenheimers. This is school work."

All the while the girls baked cookies, and Mother happily took more measurements of the bathroom, Stacy talked about the game that afternoon. "Coach Kern says he doesn't care whether we win or lose. But he wants every girl on the team to be a shining example of sportsmanship—Sister Cabrina calls it Christian behavior—to these tough babes from St. Xavier. So if one of the players calls me a dirty name or kicks me in the shin when the ref isn't looking, I will only give her a saintly smile—like so." And she demonstrated.

"That I've got to see, Katie Rose laughed.

"How you talk! I aim to show my noblest self."

Miguel stopped in. He sampled the cookies. He was all interest when Mother showed how Leo could fit in the washbowl and toilet in the small cubicle, and

where the narrow glass door would open into the bath
stall. "No room for a tub. We can barely meet speci-
fications on the shower space—My, that plumbing
inspector is giving us a bad time—by pushing out this
cupboard."

Miguel asked Stacy if she needed a ride to the game
at St. Jude's. No, she was being called for. Katie Rose
grew uneasy. Supposing he just settled down for the
afternoon. She couldn't very well say, "Don't stay,
Miguel. Because I'm looking forward to a cozy afternoon with the light of my life."

She felt great relief when Miguel finally departed.
A noisy carful honked for Stacy, and she, her box of
cookies under her arm, raced out. Ben and Mother set
out to visit some salvage yards. Mother said from the
doorway, "I hope I can find a corner medicine cabi-
net. You know, Katie Rose, I have a hankering for
something arty and unusual for wallpaper. It won't
take but a smidgeon. I'll poke around at Goodwill
too—you never know what you'll find there."

"Now, Mom, no matter what bargain you find in
clothes, don't buy anything for me."

"Oh you!" Mother said with a disgusted look.

The littles—the P.P.C.s—were still out collecting.
Cully would be at their heels. The stage was set for
"*Hamlet* for Two" with glasses, bottle-opener, bowl
of ice, plate of cookies on the low table by the couch.

Bruce came bearing two cartons of coke. Oh, it was one thing to vow to put a boy in the storeroom of your heart and go about business as usual. It was one thing to tell Jeanie he was no longer Mr. Irresistible in her life. And quite another for the boy to look at you with torment in his eyes and mutter, "Adams is playing South this afternoon." He meant, of course, that *Hamlet* was a miserable substitute.

All the more reason for his undying gratitude if she helped him over the lit hurdle in time for Mr. Jacoby's signing him up for other games. All the more reason for his asking her to go to them.

He was wearing creamy white Levis and a bulky hand-knitted sweater of the same shade. His shirt collar above it was a deep blue. Strange, that Bruce without trying always looked so breathtakingly right; and that Miguel without trying could look so mismatched and thrown-together.

It was all so perfect, this sitting beside Bruce in front of the TV while outside the March wind rattled at the picket gate. She put herself out to be helpful. She explained why Hamlet felt such vengeful fury toward the king who had been his uncle but now, married to his mother, was his stepfather.

"Laertes is Ophelia's brother. See, Ophelia is in love with Hamlet—but he's so crazy mixed up—Polonius is their father, and he's giving Laertes all this advice because he's going away. Do you realize what wonderful irony it is for Shakespeare to have gabby old Polonius say, 'Brevity is the soul of wit'?" She didn't mention that she never would have realized it herself, if Grandfather Belford hadn't once pointed it out.

Bruce drank one coke after another. He said once, "I guess Stacy's playing her tough game this afternoon."

"Yes, St. Xavier's. The game must be over about now, but they're going to have cocoa and cookies afterwards."

The play ground on. Just when Hamlet on the screen was holding the skull and giving his "Alas, poor Yorick" speech, the side door was thrown open and Stacy burst in.

She was still in her basketball togs. She stood leaning against the door, her red hair blown every whichway. She was panting for breath and crying. When Stacy cried, her tears did not fall as the gentle dew from heaven. They fell like a cloudburst.

Bruce and Katie Rose got to their feet and hurried to her. "Stacy, what happened?" she asked, and Bruce said, "Did you lose the game?"

"Yes, we lost—but—that—that's not what I'm crying for. It's because I—I— But look, you can see how swollen this ankle is. It's from her kicking me on the shin—over and over—"

Tears coursed on as she tumbled out her incoherent story. She had been guarded in the game by a girl named Olga. "I never had a guard so—so rough—so mean—"

"Didn't the ref call fouls on her?" Bruce asked.

"She had three called on her. He couldn't see all of them—she was so sneaky—"

And then when the game was over and both teams were in St. Jude's one dressing room, Olga had sneeringly asked Stacy why she was limping. One of the loyal St. Jude's had answered, "You ought to know. You're the one who kicked her all through the game," to which Olga had answered, "I'm sorry I didn't break her foot."

"Sweet-sounding character," muttered Bruce.

Stacy sobbed out, "And I—I reached out and slapped her."

"You slapped her!" Katie Rose breathed. "Didn't she—this Olga—slap you back?"

"No, she just stood there—kind of stunned. So was everybody else. So was I. And then I ran out the door without even dressing or anything. I shouldn't have. Because now I've got to go back."

"Why?" Bruce wanted to know.

"To apologize. I've got to run all the way back so's to get there before she's gone. I've got to tell Coach Kern and Sister Cabrina that I didn't really mean to.

Honest, I didn't even know I was slapping her—till my hand stung—"

There was no shaking her determination. Bruce said she certainly didn't need to run all that way back; he'd take her in his car.

"Well, come on then—let's hurry. Katie Rose, you come with me."

With Stacy giving choky directions, the three drove to the old red brick St. Jude's with its new addition of gym and lunchroom. Bruce stopped in front, and the three got out. Katie Rose said uneasily, "You should have worn a coat, Stacy." Stacy didn't seem to hear her though she was shivering and goose-fleshy in the cold wind.

Her eyes were on the school door and the steps. Evidently the good-fellowship serving of cocoa and cookies was ended, for students were now pouring out the door and down the steps. They paused as the raw March wind hit them, to pull together jackets and sweaters. The visiting St. Xavier's were easily distinguishable. Their colors were maroon and gold. St. Jude's were Kelly green and white.

Stacy muttered, "There's Olga now—just coming down the steps."

For a second or two, Stacy seemed to cringe between Katie Rose and Bruce before she started resolutely toward a girl who, at that moment, stopped to tug a wrinkled scarf out of her pocket and tie it around her untidy blond hair.

Katie Rose, a step behind Stacy, noticed that Olga was having a time of it what with a purse under one arm and basketball shoes dangling from the other wrist. She noticed too that the hulking, bushy-haired boy with her made no move to help. You'd think he would at least offer to hold her purse. Olga's head was bent as she fumbled a knot in the whipping scarf.

She was at the foot of the steps when she lifted her head and saw Stacy coming toward her. For only an instant she stiffened in rage. She screamed out a choice name then and lunged toward Stacy, her hand upraised.

Bruce was beside Stacy, and he reached out and blocked Olga's blow. Before Stacy could utter a word of apology, the boy with the bushy black hair and underslung jaw swung on Bruce. His fist caught him on the side of the head and sent him reeling.

Every student froze in his tracks—even the irate Olga and the amazed Stacy. Even Katie Rose, who heard a St. Jude student cry out, "Those Xavier's—they're fightin' bohunks."

Someone in the St. Xavier crowd yelled out in relish, "That's the stuff, Link. Let Pretty Boy have it."

Pretty Boy, Katie Rose thought in fury.

Bruce, the star athlete
of Adams High, regained his shaky footing, and gazed
around him in shocked disbelief. Another jeering,
"Did Pretty Boy get mussed up?" seemed to jolt him
into action. He swung on his assailant and landed a
hard blow on his belligerent jaw.

The fight was on. Gasps went up from onlookers at
the fury and force behind the flailing fists. Katie Rose
watched, her heart crowding her throat. Bruce was
used to boxing in the gym according to *rules*. But
there were no rules in this pummeling rough-and-
tumble. Link would back off with lowered head and
charge like a bull—or a goat—at Bruce's middle.

It wasn't right for Bruce to be drawn into a fight
when he had told her and Miguel he had never liked to
fight, that he had never seen much sense in— Her

thoughts broke off at the sight of Link using a foot movement to trip Bruce, and she screamed out, "Watch out, Bruce!" It was too late. He half fell—but he was on his feet again, and repaying Link with a slam on his head.

The two schools were now sharply divided. Each time Bruce landed a blow, St. Jude's cheered with "Smack him again." From the other side came, "Aw, did Pretty Boy get his hair mussed up!"

Both factions were now hurling insults at each other. A general free-for-all was building up, when suddenly the whole atmosphere changed. Onlookers stopped both their cheering and jeering, and stood watchful and silent. Stacy nudged Katie Rose. "Here comes Coach Kern."

Every eye was on the broad-shouldered young man in his dark slacks and turtle-neck sweater who came slowly down the steps, carrying his small canvas bag. So this was the much-quoted Andy Kern. Katie Rose longed to scream out, "Stop the fight, Coach Kern." Blood was trickling down Bruce's chin and onto his thick white sweater. He had lost a shoe in one of Link's buffeting attacks.

Coach Kern did not interfere. He stood on the bottom step, neither smiling nor unsmiling, his eyes on the two fighters who were the only ones unconscious of his presence. Katie Rose murmured, "Doesn't

St. Xavier have a coach?" and someone turned to murmur back, "Yeah, but he had to go to a funeral, so he didn't show up."

The boys fought on. Katie Rose thought she saw a flicker of approval on Coach Kern's face when again Link charged into Bruce's middle and Bruce undercut him with his fist and brought the bushy head up with a jolt. Someone commented, "Link can't see out of one eye—it's swollen shut," and Katie Rose said in a low whimper, "Stacy, just look how Bruce's lip is bleeding."

There came a moment when both boys backed away from each other. Both were wobbly on their legs, and exhausted of breath. It was then that Coach Kern stepped between them and said evenly, "Okay, fellows, let's break it up. We'll call it a draw." He unzipped his bag, pulled out a towel, and handed it to a St. Jude student. "Wet this in the fountain there and bring it back."

He used the towel impartially to dab at Link's swelling eye and to wipe the blood off Bruce's face. He asked, "Is this just a cut lip? Or have you lost a tooth?"

Bruce managed to pant out that he thought he still had all his teeth. Coach Kern said, "Link, just hold that wet towel to your eye. Now then, would you mind telling me what all this is about?"

Neither of the contestants had the breath to answer, but Stacy said nervously, "This is Bruce Seerie, Coach—and he brought me back—and Katie Rose, too. She's my sister."

The coach's deep gray eyes flicked over the disheveled Bruce, over Katie Rose as she bent to pick up Bruce's torn shoe; they rested on Stacy, her eyes still red from crying. "All right, Stacy, so Bruce came back to school with you. What I want to know is what started the fight?"

A rumble of "Link hit him first," came from the St. Jude side.

"What'd you hit him for, Link?"

Link could give him only a stupid stare out of his one uncovered eye. Olga volunteered the answer. "Link hit this Bruce—or whatever his name is—because he grabbed my arm."

"Why did he grab your arm?"

Olga hesitated on the why, but a St. Jude player answered for her, "Because she started for Stacy, and all Bruce did was stop her from hitting Stacy."

"I do believe we're getting warmer," Coach Kern said with an ironic grin. "Stacy, supposing you take it from here. Why was Olga going to wham you?"

Stacy swallowed. "Because I slapped her," she admitted in a thin, reedy voice.

A veritable chorus of defense went up from her

teammates. "But, Coach, Olga kicked her shins all through the game—every time the referee turned his back. Just look at her ankles. And then after the game Olga told Stacy she wished she had broken her foot."

Katie Rose, too, intervened in Stacy's behalf, "She didn't mean to slap her—she really didn't, Coach Kern. And she was sorry as soon as she did. She said she had to run all the way back and apologize to Olga, and that's why Bruce and I brought her back."

An uneasy silence fell while both sides waited for Coach's verdict. Now that the sun was dropping behind the mountains, the air was gray and chill. Jackets were again tugged together.

The Coach said, "I'm not going to rake you fellows over the coals about your fight. I've been in a lot worse myself. Fighting it out is a lot better than holding grudges or ill-feeling."

He looked around at the two factions, separated by the ill-feeling he spoke of. His wonderful, half-regretful smile included them all. "Do you know, St. Xavier's, that who won today wasn't important? My dad is a police captain, and I used to hear him talk about 'bad blood' between people or gangs. He'd shake his head and say, 'It's bad—this bad blood.' What we wanted today was for you to come out here as friends, play a basketball game, and leave as friends."

Stacy looked as though she would gladly have

crawled into a hole if there had been one to crawl into. Olga was again working at knotting the scarf under her chin and didn't look up.

Coach Kern added, "I was counting on—we all were—on being asked to your school for a return game."

There was an uneasy stirring in the St. Xavier unit, and a girl's voice said, "Well, we—we were counting on it, too. Our coach told us to ask you." A muttered argument between the team, and then, "We think it's three weeks from today, our coach said."

"Swell," the St. Jude coach said. Again that one-with-you grin. "Should we bring our own Band-Aids and Mercurochrome?"

Both sides tittered. And the laugh somehow broke the tension and animosity. "All right, boys and girls, it's getting toward suppertime," Coach Kern went on. "Let's be on our way. Now has everyone got transportation?"

Everybody nodded.

When Link handed the towel back to the coach with a muttered thanks, he said brusquely, "No, wet it again in cold water and hold it over your eye on the ride home. Did you drive the car over? Well, have someone else drive it back."

As the crowd began to disperse he called out to the

St. Xavier team, "By the way, I want one of you to explain to your coach what happened. Olga, how about your doing that?"

She was walking off with Link. She turned, barely darted a look their way, and nodded without a word.

Coach Kern murmured on a chuckle, "A girl of action and few words."

He *is* wonderful, Katie Rose thought. He didn't overdo the making of peace between the two factions. He didn't even suggest that Link and Bruce shake hands, or demand that Stacy apologize to Olga for slapping her.

He shooed off the St. Jude students who would have lingered with Stacy to postmortem it all. All the cars pulled away until only Bruce's convertible and a station wagon with the lettering "St. Joseph's Seminary" on it were left.

The handkerchief Bruce held to his mouth was spotted with red. So was his near-white sweater with its lumpy popcorn stitch. "I hope that sweater is washable, Bruce," Coach Kern said.

Bruce answered thickly but cheerfully, "I don't think so. Mom says they keep their shape better to send them to the cleaner's."

Andy Kern reached over and carefully felt Bruce's jaw, pressed his nose. "That's wonderful. No missing teeth, no broken nose, no dislocated jaw. I noticed that uppercut you used. Pretty neat."

A waiting silence fell. Stacy shivered convulsively, and Katie Rose took off her jacket and drew it over both their shoulders. And still Coach Kern stood thoughtfully and gently swinging his canvas bag.

Stacy ventured in a shaky voice, "Does Sister Cabrina know about—about—?"

"Your whacking Olga? Oh yes, she knows. That was the slap heard round the school."

"What's she going to do—about—about me?"

"She told me you had slapped yourself right off the team."

A strangled sob came from Stacy. And both Katie Rose and Bruce started with, "But she didn't mean—"

Coach Kern held up his hand. "Wait—wait. I told her I thought that was too severe, that two weeks off the team would be punishment enough."

"Should I go in and see her now?" Stacy asked, shivering worse than ever.

"Not now, Stacy. Right now she's pretty hot under the wimple. You wait till Monday. You go on home. Trim up a Band-Aid and fit it over that cut on Bruce's lip. Get on with you."

His car was parked in the driveway. The three

turned as they reached the convertible. He was still standing there, and he lifted his hand in farewell. It was like a blessing.

"Good egg," Bruce muttered through the spotted handkerchief.

"You get in the middle," Katie Rose told Stacy. Her heart went out to poor chastened Stacy whose spasmodic shivers were like held-back sobs. She said as the car started, "Golly, Bruce, it was—all my fault— and I'm sorry I got you into that—that fight."

"You needn't be." He swung around the corner with a flourish. "Did you hear someone call me Pretty Boy? That's what geared me for action." He threw back his head and laughed. "I'll bet that black-haired ape that swung on me won't be able to see out of his left eye tomorrow."

The girls laughed shakily, and Katie Rose said, "Not for a week, I'll bet."

They were turning onto Hubbell when Stacy said, "I'll catch holy Ned from Mom and Ben—oh, and Sister Cabrina on Monday, and maybe Father Lambert too. But I won't mind any of that—not as much, I mean—as being put off—off the team—" and she dropped her head on Katie Rose's shoulder and cried afresh.

Katie Rose patted her and tried to comfort her,

"Just don't say a word back to Sister Cabrina. I remember how if we always just stood there looking sorrowful and said, 'Yes, Sister. No, Sister,' she wasn't so bad."

The Belford house sat on the corner facing on Hubbell Street. The family and frequent callers never stopped in front of the house, and came to the front door; they pulled up to the curb at the side, and went through the picket gate and to the door that opened into the dining room. Heretofore, Bruce had always stopped in front. This windy and chill dusk, as though feeling a new intimacy, he turned off Hubbell and stopped at the side gate.

Mother and Ben were not home yet. The littles were. They looked at the battle-scarred Bruce with wondrous respect. They hunted up salve for his skinned knuckles. They offered to take his ripped loafer to the shoemaker's. "If we tell him you need it right away, he'll stitch it up while we wait."

"No, that's all right. I've got another pair at home."

While Katie Rose fitted a small rectangle of Band-Aid over the cut on his lip, Jill offered him advice. "Look, Bruce, when you double your fist up, leave the thumb sticking out like this— And that way you can gouge, gouge with it while you're hitting."

"It don't always work," Matt said wisely. "Because

sometimes, somebody you're fighting bites your thumb."

Again Bruce threw back his head and laughed. Strange, this new exultant and cocky Bruce. Katie Rose hadn't heard him laugh like that since—well, since the Monday he came out of that fateful session in Mr. Knight's office.

"Stacy," he asked, "what was the score in the game you lost to St. Xavier's this afternoon?"

"Eighteen to fifteen. I just couldn't seem to make the free throws. Just think, if I'd scored on the fouls Olga made, we'd have won," she grieved.

"You need more practice. Practice twirling the ball just as it leaves your hands—putting a little English on it, they call it. I worked on it for hours on end."

"I wish I could." Stacy still looked chilled and woebegone. She said, "Katie Rose, make some tea right away. And when Mom and Ben come home, give Mom a cup of tea first. And, you littles, don't you be spilling out about—about my slapping Olga—till she has two cups."

"Oh, we won't," they vowed.

Bruce wouldn't wait for tea. He wanted to take his blotchy sweater to the cleaners on the Boulevard before it closed. "Just as well for Mom not to see it."

Katie Rose watched him through the gate, the roll

of sweater under his arm. She watched him drive off. He backed up and turned at the corner with that same cock-of-the-walk flourish. Yes, strange! He had been so sunk in bitterness against life. You'd think getting bruised and bloodied in a fight would make him more so.

8

Monday at school was a delightsome day. (*Delightsome* was another of Stacy's words, but Miguel wouldn't let Katie Rose correct her. It was a dictionary word, he said.)

First, Mrs. Dujardin was back. Katie Rose was putting her wraps in her locker when she saw her in the hall and hurried to her to say how glad she was that she was over her sick spell and back at school.

The drama teacher was a big woman with flashing black eyes and a commanding presence. This morning she looked drained and pale from her week of illness.

"I'm glad to be back, Katie Rose. I worried about being off a week with the tryouts coming up. We'll have to get right to them. I was telling Ned—Mr. Hill—that we'll take you and Zoe first."

Katie Rose's heart lifted high. To be classed with Zoe

who was as close to professional as a schoolgirl could be! She had danced a ballet number in last summer's opera.

"I'll be ready any time, Mrs. Dujardin. I can come before school or stay after."

Mrs. Dujardin patted her arm. "You're nice to work with, my dear."

Katie Rose couldn't wait to tell Jeanie about Mrs. Dujardin linking her and Zoe together. Jeanie said gaily, "Katie Rose, you're in like Flynn."

Her heart lifted high again when she came out of math at midmorning and found Bruce waiting for her. His bruised knuckles were taped, and his lower lip was puffed out of shape. But there was nothing of last week's moodiness about him as he took her arm and walked with her to Madame Miller's French class. "I've been wondering about Stacy. What did your mom and Ben say?"

"Oh, they weren't too rough on her. They knew she'd catch it today from Sister Cabrina. What about you? What did your folks say about the fight?"

He laughed. "They said plenty, but I didn't care. You know what I did, Katie Rose? I reread *Hamlet* from that poor-Yorick bit on. It wasn't bad there at the last where they fought a duel with one of the sword tips poisoned. I had sort of a fellow feeling for that dopey Hamlet. Now I have to tackle *Hiawatha*."

He left her at the door of the French class with, "I'll be waiting for you after school."

After school, she again told Miguel and Jeanie that Bruce badly needed help on "New Impressions of *Hamlet*" for Mr. Jacoby, and raced to the parking lot and Bruce's car. Bruce didn't head for the Boulevard and Downey's but drove straight to Hubbell Street. Just as she was wondering about asking him in when all the plumbing was in progress, he leaped out of the car. "I'm anxious to know what they dished out to Stacy at school today."

They walked into the smell of hot metal and the hiss of an acetylene torch. The only visible part of Leo was his feet extending from the part of the closet that would be the shower. Mother was holding a coffee can of patching plaster and a smeary pancake turner.

She greeted them with a tired, busy smile. "A pancake turner is handy for smoothing on plaster as well as flipping pancakes and swatting kids."

"Is Stacy home yet?" Katie Rose asked.

"I'm in here," Stacy called.

She was sitting at the dining table surrounded by sheets of notebook paper, some blank and some covered with her large handwriting.

"What did your Sister Cabrina say?" Bruce wanted to know.

Stacy answered by holding up a page. "I have to

write this five hundred times and hand it in to her."
They looked over her shoulder to read:

"I lost my temper and brought dishonor to
St. Jude's school. *Mea culpa, mea culpa, mea
maxima culpa.*"

"What does that *mea* stuff mean?" he asked.

" 'Through my fault, through my fault, through
my most grievous fault.' And besides this, when all the
basketball team goes in to practice in the gym—" she
took a minute to straighten her lips, "I have to go into
church and say a rosary."

"I think that's pretty stiff," Bruce said feelingly.

"What about Father Lambert?" Katie Rose asked.
"Did you have to see him too?"

Stacy shook back her tears. "Yes, but he's such a
sweetie. He just asked me how I'd like to recite the
Lord's Prayer if it said, 'Forgive us our trespasses as
we slap those who trespass against us,' and I couldn't
help but laugh—and he laughed too. How many
times does eight go into five hundred, Bruce?"

He gave a moment to mental arithmetic. "I get
sixty-two and a half."

"That's how many pages it'll take to turn in to
Sister Cabrina. See, I can only write it eight times on
one sheet."

Bruce looked at her wonderingly. "Aren't you

pretty griped and sore about all this? About their pouring it on you like that?"

She shook her reddish blond pony tail slowly. "I had it coming to me. And it'll be so delightsome when I get back on the team."

Mother called in to ask Bruce to stay and have a cup of tea with them. He thanked her but said no, he guessed he'd better get home and study. Katie Rose walked to the door with him. He surprised her by asking, "You remember that day we went to your grandfather's, and he mentioned some poem—it said something about not whimpering. Do you remember who wrote it?"

"Walt Whitman. 'Henceforth, I whimper no more, postpone no more.' " She was always happy when she could show him how much she knew in lit or poetry.

"Thanks, Katie Rose," he said absently.

She was glad he hadn't stayed. For it developed that everyone had to wash his own cup and drink his tea standing, because the dinette table and benches were piled high with odd lengths of plasterboard.

At supper that evening Katie Rose told the family about the tryouts for Mrs. Dujardin's musical comedy. "You know how super Zoe is? And Mrs. Du said she'd try her and me out first. Howard told Deetsy and Deetsy told me that we could choose our own numbers for the tryout."

Stacy said, "Oh, Katie Rose, do 'I Could Dance All Night,' and then break into that soft-shoe step Uncle Brian taught us. That'd be a knockout."

"I was thinking I might."

Mother said, "The music for it is in the piano bench. You'd better take it with you." And Leo said, "I've got my tools piled on it. Come on, Katie Rose, and I'll lift them off for you."

When she went to study hall the next day, Mr. Jacoby showed her the slip which excused her for her tryout in the auditorium. She left on Jeanie's, "Good luck!" and Miguel's, "May heaven *and* Mrs. Dujardin smile on you, Katie Petunia."

She fought against stagefright as she hurried down the hall, opened the heavy doors into the auditorium, and started the long walk toward the stage. How empty and awesome and echoing this vast space seemed when all the hundreds of seats were vacant. Her vocal music teacher, Mr. Hill, was turning on the light over the piano that slanted out from the stage. Mrs. Dujardin and Howard were talking beside it.

Zoe was there too and, like Katie Rose, had a roll of music.

Zoe came from an "acting family." Howard had told Deetsy, and Deetsy passed the information on to their lunch table, that Zoe's mother was touring the country in a road show. Deetsy had also added, "You'd think Zoe could dress better."

Today she was wearing a striped blouse that seemed too large on her slim shoulders and a straight skirt that was twisted halfway around on her. Sometimes her long and heavy ash-blond hair was caught back with a wispy ribbon; sometimes she wore it in a braid thick as a wrist. Today it was braided. Her face was as thin as an elf's, and her eyes, the color of amber, seemed almost too large for her face.

She was never chatty. But she knew more "theater" than anyone in their drama class. Katie Rose liked her for her very differentness. "Have you tried out yet, Zoe?" she asked shakily, as she deposited her books and took the seat next to her.

"Not yet," Zoe whispered back. "I'm scared too. Oh, our music, we'd better flatten it out."

. . . Grandda O'Byrne, the onetime Abbey player, always said, "Every actor worth his salt has stagefright so bad he can't spit, until he gets on the stage and says his first line or takes one dance step, and then— why, then he's more at home than in his own old rocker." . . .

Mrs. Dujardin was saying, "You first, Zoe. Just a song. We already know you can dance, and I've heard you take a speaking part."

Zoe conferred hastily with the voice teacher and

handed him her music. She hurried up the three steps onto the stage. Howard turned on the footlights.

Zoe sang "How Are Things in Glocca Morra?" Her voice had a certain flat and husky timbre that reached out movingly. Listening to her, Katie Rose had a feeling that Zoe was confiding her aching nostalgia for a willow tree, as though she were begging, "Tell me— only tell me—is that willow tree still weeping there?"

No wonder she had been the first one Mrs. Dujardin tried out. No wonder Mrs. Dujardin met her at the foot of the stage steps at the song's end, and beamed at her. "That's wonderful, Zoe. You get on back to your sewing class now. I'm glad we have your talent to count on for our show."

That was as good as saying, "You'll get one of the leads."

The drama teacher motioned to Katie Rose then. She was still flattening the sheet music she had brought, and she said nervously, "I'm going to sing that song from *My Fair Lady*."

The boyish Mr. Hill reached for the music. "I'm glad you brought this. After all our practicing *Hosanna* for Easter, I just might launch into that on my own. Want me to play this straight through, and then repeat the chorus?"

"Yes, please, Mr. Hill."

The auditorium looked more vast and frightening than ever from the stage. . . . Grandda O'Byrne had also told Katie Rose summer before last when she played in a show he directed, "Forget who you are, and become the part you're playing." . . .

And she did. With her first swaying waltz steps, her first "Oh, I could dance—" she became not Katie Rose who had been excused from study hall, but a girl who had just come home from her first ball. She became that girl, dressed not in a purple jumper and lavender blouse, but an enraptured girl in a long, voluminous and shimmering white evening gown. Even Katie Rose's scuffed flats turned into fragile gold slippers on her feet.

She sang it as she waltzed through it once, and then she broke into the soft-shoe step in three-quarter time Uncle Brian had drilled her in. She glided out of it in time for the final glad, "I could dance, dance, dance all night."

She could tell they were pleased. Mrs. Dujardin and Mr. Hill smiled at her, and then at each other. Howard said, "Aren't you the one—breaking into that slip-slap step to waltz time. Where'd you ever learn that?"

He didn't wait for an answer but walked up on the stage to join her. He was shuffling through some mimeographed sheets, and he asked Mrs. Dujardin, "What do you want her to read—the Anna Lucasta part, or Ophelia?"

Katie Rose held her breath. Ophelia would be a break. Hadn't she sat and watched the poor tortured girl who loved Hamlet on the TV screen last Saturday?

"Ophelia will be fine. Only skip that long speech by Polonius, Howard."

He handed Katie Rose two of the sheets. "I'll feed you the lines, and you come in as Ophelia. Can you see all right?"

"Oh yes."

This was the scene where the meek Ophelia was catechised by both her brother and her father over Lord Hamlet and his avowals of love.

Howard demanded,

"What is between you? Give me up the truth."

And she answered,

"He hath, my lord, of late made many tenders
Of his affection to me. . . ."

Howard was just saying with angry emphasis,

"You have taken these tenders for true pay,
Which are not sterling. Tender yourself more
dearly. . . ."

when the first passing bell rang.

Mrs. Dujardin interrupted, "That's enough anyway. I only wanted to hear your speaking voice, Katie Rose." She reached out her hand to Katie Rose as she came down the steps from the stage. "Very good, child, very good. You have that same quality Zoe has of reaching out to the audience. Your voice carries well, too."

The orchestra teacher had come through the stage door. He pushed up to Mrs. Dujardin and, gesturing with his glasses, began explaining how the scores for certain musical comedies would be far beyond reach of his students. Mrs. Dujardin knit her brows as she listened.

Katie Rose lingered, hoping the drama teacher would turn her attention to her just long enough to say, as she had to Zoe, "I'm glad we have your talent to count on for the show."

The final bell rang and Katie Rose could only snatch up her books, her mother's music from the piano, and go racing down the hall to Room 113 and Mr. Jacoby's class in lit.

When the class was over she thanked him for letting her leave study hall for her tryout.

"I was glad to. I suppose you'll have a part in the musicale? If I were casting, I'd give you one. You've got leading lady ingredients—winsome, flowerlike, but with fire in your veins."

Well, he certainly was in an expansive mood! Out

of her excited happiness, she confided, "I'm helping Bruce Seerie get caught up in lit."

He gave her a sharp look. "What do you mean by *helping* him, Kathleen?"

She said hastily, "I'm not doing any of his work for him. But you see, I never would have understood some of the underlying meanings in *The Old Man and the Sea* or *Lost Horizon* if I hadn't heard Father or Grandfather Belford talking about them. I even took Bruce to Grandfather's because he knows so much about poetry." She laughed in memory. "And talks so much about it."

Mr. Jacoby laughed with her. "I know. I know your grandfather. We have one thing in common. We both think Tennyson's a sweetsop—only don't quote me on that because there're some who think his 'Crossing the Bar' is right up there with the Beatitudes."

And then his face sobered. "About Bruce, Kathleen, and my failing him. I'm not keeping him off the team out of meanness. Oh, I know the stock remark of teachers is that it isn't fair to other students to pass someone who can't make the grade. But I also say it isn't fair to a student to let him slide by. He's being cheated if you let him go on thinking that literature and poetry are in the same class with embroidery or hymn singing—something for the sissies, but not for football players. That attitude enrages me."

"It's just that lit is hard for Bruce," she defended.

"It's just that he's always closed his pores to it. Bruce's life is bounded on the north, south, east, and west by being good in sports. He's insulated. So, Kathleen, if you can get through that insulation and somehow bring out a little sensitivity to the written word —well, you deserve a medal."

Katie Rose couldn't wait to call her Uncle Brian at his San Francisco apartment that evening, and tell him about her tryout. He was Mother's youngest brother, and a lovable, redheaded man with his tongue dripping blarney. It was he who had taught Katie Rose, Ben and Stacy to dance the Irish jig and sing all the old ballads.

She said when he picked up the phone, "It's Katie Rose, Uncle Brian."

He said on a delighted whoop, "Mavourneen, my dear love, my bright angel. It's a treat to hear your voice."

He was all interest in her telling about her tryout. He was sure she would be given the lead. "So they liked our soft-shoe variation. What play are they putting on?"

"They don't know yet. I think they have to find a musical comedy the school orchestra can handle."

He told her of his joining the Lady Gregory players

in San Francisco. "One of these days we'll arrange for you to visit me. It's proud I'll be to introduce you to them. And we'll show them—you and I , bright angel —how the Irish jig ought to be danced."

She hung up the phone in quivery, deep-seated happiness. Oh, what beautiful days this second Monday and Tuesday in March had been!

"The sun, my proud beauties, is now past the frozen arctic," Miguel announced, as they halted at their seats in study hall on Thursday. "Now it's aiming at your elbow, Petunia."

The proud beauties smiled absently, each absorbed in her thoughts.

Jeanie was one of the sophomore reporters on the school paper. She had a gift for versifying, and she had told their crowd at lunch that the editor wanted her to write up the school's impromptu dance the day before in rhyme. She sat down at her desk, pulled a sheet of paper toward her, and began writing swiftly.

Katie Rose's absent smile was because she was still in a joyful trance of reliving the dance Jeanie was writing about. She looked across and read Jeanie's deft and legible printing:

> *"Our dance on Wednesday afternoon*
> *Came to us as a special boon*
> *From Mr. Knight—three cheers for him!—*
> *And was held as always in our spacious gym."*

In yesterday's assembly Mr. Knight had announced that the Lowry Air Force orchestra could come that afternoon to play dance music. He had to hold up his hand to silence the loud cheers. "I had a feeling the natives were getting restless with all work and no play," he said with a fond smile. More whoops and cheers to be silenced before he added, "But remember, this is to be a *mixer,* not a pairing-off affair."

He always made that point. As all the school knew, he had a *thing* about everybody dancing with everybody else. He had said yesterday, as he had so often, "You'll have a long stretch of being paired off in marriage later on. This is the 'getting to know you' time in your life."

But Katie Rose had danced the first dance with Bruce, and the second with Bruce who could talk about his make-up work in lit without ever getting out of step. And then—wouldn't you know!— Mr. Knight had boomed out over the speaker, "Everybody change partners." She had danced with Miguel who, whether he talked or kept silent, was seldom in step with the music. She had danced with Bruce again.

Now she opened her Prose and Poetry book, and drew out the pages she had written on the life of Katie Rose. But her ball-point pen, unlike Jeanie's, didn't fly. It doodled. There was such a thing as a writer being so enrapt with life, she couldn't write about it. She couldn't put down for Mr. Jacoby's perusal:

"Life is so wonderful, so beautiful. I am Bruce's guide and inspiration. Because of me, he now appreciates Walt Whitman and Hamlet. I will always have a special place in his heart."

Mr. Jacoby's attention was given to a student who had gone up to his desk to confer with him. Jeanie took that chance to ask Katie Rose *sotto voce*, "Why was Deetsy so grumpy at the dance?"

Katie Rose answered in like manner, "Hunger, *and* her Howie's dancing with Zoe."

Deetsy had, indeed, been grumpy. Their lunch-room group had gravitated together between dances, and it was then that Deetsy said to Katie Rose, "Can you imagine any mother naming a baby a crazy name like Zoe?"

There was that in Katie Rose that always rose to the defense of anyone under attack. "Sure I can. And Zoe is just right for her."

"She's always fastening herself on Howie. She came down from drama with him, so of course he feels like he has to dance with her. She's so stuck-up because she's danced in summer opera."

"She isn't a bit stuck-up. She's real friendly when you get to know her."

Another girl had walked from a classroom and into the gym with a boy. That, too, drew an unhappy barb from Deetsy. "There's your brother Ben, Katie Rose. Gollee, who's that freak he's with?"

"That's Grace. She's his partner in biology lab, and she isn't a freak. Ben says she's the smartest girl he ever knew."

"If she's so smart she ought to know better than to wear yellow when her skin is already yellowish."

Next Deetsy called Katie Rose's attention to Jeanie. "When she isn't dancing with Ben, she's dancing with her new love. See that little shorty who's always hanging around your locker."

Katie Rose's eyes sought out Jeanie in the brown-checked skirt she had made in sewing, and the cinnamon-colored sweater that matched her hair and eyes. Her partner was certainly not the Lochinvar type. He was a little taller than Jeanie. He always wore a droll, untroubled smile, as though he and life shared some secret joke.

"Jeanie says he's a poet, and she calls him Robert Burns," Deetsy contributed further.

"His last name *is* Burns, and he's on the paper staff with her," Katie Rose said shortly. She gave Deetsy a condemning look and turned away from her.

But Deetsy caught her arm, and her face suddenly crumpled. "Katie Rose, I'm so hungry. You just can't help being mean when you're hollow as a gourd inside."

"Well for Pete's sake, Deetsy, eat a candy bar or something."

"I would if I had one," she confessed humbly.

"Here's half of one Miguel gave me in study. Maybe that'll improve your outlook on life. You, and your cottage cheese."

Deetsy had one saving grace: her candor. No matter how her constant chatter irritated the lunch bunch it was her appealing honesty that won them back, just as it did Katie Rose when Deetsy said around her crunching of the half a candy bar, "I'm such a dope. When Howie said Zoe was like a sylph, I thought I could be too. And look at the mess my hair is just because I tried to make it as blond as June's. I wish I were as smart and pretty as you are, Katie Rose. No wonder Bruce is so wild about you."

On that, Katie Rose forgave her her grumpiness and her gossip.

Everyone had mixed at Mr. Knight's mixer. Katie Rose danced with the John-Toms, and they told her they had mixed the red paint she donated for Delia's coat of many colors with some donated blue, and come out with a passionate mauve. She danced with Freddy who was in her math class. He told her as he always did that he'd like to teach her to ski. "You will never know ecstasy until you take off down a snowy slope."

She already knew ecstasy. (Ec-*stacy*, Stacy called it.) Her pen wanted to write,

"Bruce told me he heard I was getting one of the leads in the school play, and that he'd be in the front row."

Mr. Jacoby was rapping on his desk for attention. "You students who are working on the story of your life, let me call your attention to that one suggestion on your slip: 'What is your heart's desire?' I have just been asked if I meant the tangible or the intangible. Both. If you crave new skin-diving apparatus, or maybe a leopard coat, that's something tangible. But your intangible desires are even more interesting be-

cause they're a part of the you I want to come alive in
your paper."

Katie Rose left off her doodling long enough to
write,

"*If there's one thing I crave it's a phone extension
in the bedroom I share with Stacy upstairs. It would
make life a little more private. My life is so unprivate.*"

She could even write,

"*My heart's desire is to have a part in the school
play because it will be a stepping stone to my becoming an actress.*"

Dreams took over. She was seeing herself on the
stage here at Adams High, carrying the audience with
her. And among the loudest clappers would be an im-
pressed—even awed—Bruce Seerie. She saw herself
taking a last curtain call. She heard feet running up
the aisle, as some lesser minion brought her a bouquet
of roses. Wasn't it always roses that admirers sent to
actresses? Yes, a great sheaf of long-stemmed roses,
because money was no object to Bruce—well, not as
much as it would be to Miguel or the John-Toms, or
even Freddy with all his big talk about taking her
skiing.

Jeanie turned and whispered to Miguel, "Can you
think of anything to rhyme with *orchestra?*"

"Nothing will. Change it to *band* and then it'll rhyme with 'We gave them a hand' or 'The music was grand.' "

The bell rang. Jeanie said, "I want to finish it with something like '—came the end of the ball, and a wonderful—' or maybe gorgeous or delightful 'time was had by all.' "

"Or maybe *delightsome*," suggested Katie Rose.

At school's closing on Friday, she came down the stairs from choir practice. Miguel and Jeanie were waiting at the lockers, and Katie Rose sang out in high spirits, "Hallelujah! Hallelujah!"

They chanted it with her. Other students at other lockers picked it up, banging metal doors in rhythm, "Hallelujah!—this is Friday," until the math teacher passed by and silenced them with a look of disapproval.

Miguel said, "Get into your mackinaw, Petunia. We are about to perfect your driving technique. Gramps is getting picky since he's been laid up with his cast. He wants some strictly fresh eggs, and Jeanie knows where we can get some by taking a four- or five-mile drive." He fixed her with a threatening eye. "And one word out of you, my pet, about having to be a savior to Bruce, and I'll blow a gasket."

She laughed and said, "Let's have no gasket-blowing."

She was not being Bruce's savior today. At the drinking fountain this morning he had told her that he would be hurrying from school to the airport to meet a friend of his mother's. "Mom has to lead a Great Books discussion—or symposium or whatever."

"I'll be home tomorrow afternoon, Bruce. I'm baby-sitting for some folks who're going out to dinner, but I won't be leaving until around four. So if you need any help—"

He wasn't sure. This same visitor might be catching a plane, and his folks might wish her off on him again.

"Make it if you can," she said, trying to keep her eagerness from showing. "We can talk over *Hiawatha*." She didn't tell him she had devoted a whole evening to rereading it, and marking significant passages for him.

Jeanie said as they threaded their way through the parking lot, "I wish I could go with you two. But I have to scan my so-called poetry, type it, and turn it in at a staff meeting tonight."

Miguel was driving not his old and weathered little Mercedes-Benz today, but his grandfather's Dodge. "Get in the driver's seat, Petunia," he told her.

She got out of the parking lot without having to back or turn; she hadn't learned that yet. She drove to Harmony Heights, and to the Kincaids' white ranch house with its rosy tiled roof and pink door. Jeanie said, "Now come next door with me, and Beany Buell can tell you how to get where you're going for your new-laid eggs. It's a farm where her brother Johnny Malone and his wife live."

Katie Rose already knew Beany Buell who had been Beany Malone until last June when she married Carlton Buell. The Buells had bought the smaller house to the north of the Kincaids' last December. Jeanie had told Katie Rose how the initial payment had taken all their capital. "That's why they can't buy carpeting or new furniture."

"They've got a cherry red love seat," Katie Rose had said, and she and Jeanie laughed together over a couple having a love seat but no dining table or chairs.

Katie Rose also knew that Beany was expecting her baby next month.

She answered Jeanie's ring at the door. Miguel was introduced, and Jeanie explained that he was seeking fresh eggs and needed directions to get to Johnny's and Miggs's farm.

Beany walked out and toward the car with them. Katie Rose had heard the term "heavy with child." But somehow, even though Beany's maternity dress was crowded for room, the term *heavy* didn't fit. For she walked with a springy lightness as though the burden she carried was a joyous one.

"You turn off the highway just south of the university," she pointed. "You know where the junction is where the four-lane goes south? But you take the turn west toward the mountains. Their farm is in what they call the apple orchard district. You'll come to a wide gateway—but no gate to open—and over the gateway it says 'Carmody.' That's because Johnny married Miggs Carmody."

Jeanie put in, "Beany, tell Katie Rose and Miguel about their baby. She's a little girl—not three months yet—and they named her Melody, a combination of Malone and Carmody. Only tell them what Johnny said."

"Johnny's such a goof-ball. He said they couldn't decide between Malady, Caramel, or Melody."

Jeanie prompted again, "Tell them about Miggs's folks being so rich and how—"

"How Johnny has to fight them off?" Beany laughed again. "You should hear Johnny tell it. Miggs's father is a rich oil man in Texas, and Miggs is an only child. Johnny said that part of the wedding ceremony was for Miggs to say, 'I promise to love, honor, and obey, and take no help from my folks.' They both stand pat on it. Miggs gets such a wallop out of selling eggs from her hens, and churning butter and selling it."

Jeanie prodded further, "Tell them about the elegant bassinet Miggs's folks sent the baby."

Beany laughed ruefully. "I guess the Carmodys figure the baby is exempt from Johnny's no-gift dictum. This bassinet—all padded satin, lace canopy and rubber-tired wheels—does look out of place in their rambling old farmhouse, sitting beside a coal stove. But there, you two better go on before the sun drops lower and shines in your eyes as you go west."

They said their good-bys, and Katie Rose drove off. She always felt more confidence in her driving with Miguel than with Ben. With Miguel, her stop for a red light was never a rocking jerk. With him, she felt at one with the car. She worked her way into the traffic on the highway, and took the turn west without mishap. Miguel said, "As your teacher, I'll give you A-plus on driving. I'll watch for the gateway and sign."

The sun was still high over the mountains when Katie Rose turned off the main road through the gateway and onto a lane that led to the farmhouse.

They had no sooner stopped than a nondescript dog raced toward them, barking lustily. A young woman came from one of the farm buildings. So this was Miggs. She wore a plaid wool shirt and faded Levis with the knees about to go. The short apron was gathered in her hand. Katie Rose's grandmother in Bannon always used her apron for carrying eggs too.

Miguel, who had never yet met a stranger, hurried toward her introducing himself and Katie Rose, and peered into the apron. "Eggs. We came to the right place."

You could tell that Miggs's tan was not the kind she worked at. Her short brown hair was sun and weather bleached. Her smile was not as wide as Beany Buell's, but more shy and uncertain.

She ushered them into an unusually large and homey kitchen. The fragrant spicy smell that greeted them came from a pan of gingerbread that still sat on the oven door.

Katie Rose and Miguel helped her take the eggs from her apron and put them in cartons. "Some of them are still warm," Miguel said in surprise. "Wait'll I tell grandpop that these eggs are so fresh the hens haven't even missed them yet."

Miggs's chuckle was shy too. "I was churning but I had to leave it to gather the eggs while the baby was asleep." She motioned to the glass churn nearby. "The butter is about to come."

"Come?" queried Miguel. "Where does it come from?"

Katie Rose answered from her wisdom acquired on Bannon visits, "It comes from the sour cream, you goon."

Miguel insisted on finishing the churning. He watched with little-boy interest while Miggs scooped it out of the buttermilk with a wooden ladle into a wooden bowl. She asked, "Do you like fresh buttermilk?"

"I'm sure I do," Miguel said, "though I don't remember ever sampling it."

He tipped the churn and filled the pitcher Miggs held.

The door was thrown open and Johnny Malone came in. He was a tall young man with twinkling brown eyes and thick brown hair that looked as though it needed cutting. He appealed to the two visitors as though he had known them all his life, "Buttermilk, eh! Some little gremlin told me to drive like mad coming home because Miggs was churning. And gingerbread, too." He tossed his briefcase on a chair, and quite unashamedly drew Miggs into his arms and kissed her.

It was his presence that turned their eating gingerbread and drinking buttermilk at the kitchen table into a party. Miguel looked around the room and said, "By gosh, I've just decided; when I get married I'm going to have a big kitchen with a rocking chair and sofa in it like this."

"Kitchen!" Johnny Malone reproved. "This, if you please, is the foyer, the living room, snack bar, and dressing room on cold mornings." He indicated the set in the corner and added, "Also the TV room."

"It's about to become a nursery," Miggs said in her quiet way. "I hear stirrings from the bassinet. I'll wheel it out."

Katie Rose was on her feet. "Oh, let me. Melody is the one I've been wanting to see."

Yes, the bassinet with all its profusion of lace and pink satin—and gruntings and mumblings in its depths—did add a luxurious but not a jarring note to the big shabby room.

"We sometimes call her Cacophony," her father said. "There's nothing melodious about her when she's hungry. She has her own built-in clock that tells her when it's time to nurse."

"It isn't time yet," Miggs said.

This was the nicest part of the visit for Katie Rose. She held the baby in the kitchen while Miggs "worked" the butter in the wooden bowl. In the next room Johnny showed Miguel the pictures he had taken for his coming TV show. His program consisted of a weekly series on the industries that had built up the state.

"Our littles were just crazy about the one on cattle raising and the cowboys," Katie Rose told Miggs.

"He's done one on farming, too. Next week it's on finding oil. Johnny uses what's supposed to be the parlor for his darkroom. This is just an old farmhouse, you know, and laid off kind of crazy to begin with."

Katie Rose's attention was on the baby in her arms. She had Johnny's brown eyes. They caught the smile in Katie Rose's, and a wondering smile came over the round, pink face. Not content with the smile, she gave a gurgling crow.

"Listen to her laugh," she said to Miguel and Johnny as they came into the kitchen. "She's young to laugh out loud like that. I've been around a lot of babies, but they hardly ever laugh when they're only three months."

"She only laughs for certain people. At other times she's a sobersides," Miggs said. "I guess you know more about babies than I do. Oh look, she can't take her eyes off you. She thinks you're pretty."

"She thinks right," Miguel said.

Little Melody groped for Katie Rose's hand and her flower-petal fingers fastened on one of hers.

A wave of wondrous content—even ecstasy— swept through Katie Rose. Life couldn't be sweeter. It wasn't only that she was so necessary to Bruce and so sure of a place in his heart. It was a culmination of everything. She would go home and Mother would show her the progress of the new bath. Any day now at school the play would be announced, and the parts would be posted in the greenroom.

She looked at the three in the kitchen and the words bubbled over, "I'm so glad I came. I love being here." She could have added, "I love you all. I love life."

Miggs gave a low laugh and bent over to kiss her. "We're so glad you came too."

Saturday at noon Katie
Rose answered the telephone. It was Mrs. Purdum.

Both Katie Rose and Stacy had regular customers
for baby-sitting. Katie Rose had the Barton family
where there was an arthritic grandma they didn't like
to leave alone. She had the McHargs in their pretty,
well-kept ranch house in Harmony Heights, and their
two pretty, well-trained little girls.

Stacy had the Novak family across the street. She
also baby-sat a ten-year-old boy who was so adored
and pampered by his parents and grandparents that
she always referred to him as "the Prince."

But the one baby-sitting job which neither she nor
Stacy relished was at the Purdums'. Not only were
there four unmanageable, undisciplined little Purdum
boys, ranging from a toddler to a first-grader, but
Mrs. Purdum herself was a harassed, disorganized per-

son who expected a baby-sitter to bring order out of chaos when she herself couldn't.

Once when Stacy had substituted for Katie Rose there, she had been hacked on the shin with a coping saw. Once Katie Rose had been bitten on the thumb. Not only that, but one of the tennis shoes she was wearing this Saturday when she answered the phone, still bore faint traces of "William J. Purdum. William J—" One baby-sitting night a little Purdum had spilled a glass of milk on it, and while it was drying on the oven door, with Katie Rose busy elsewhere in the house, the enterprising Purdums had used their father's inked signature stamp on it.

On the phone Mrs. Purdum, breathless and beset as usual and with a noisy background din, took a round-about way to get to her point. "It's such a lovely day —honestly, isn't it amazing to have a March day just like May or June?—and Bill—" (William J.) "—thought it'd be wonderful for us to drive up in the foothills. He says it'll do me good to get away from the children—they've all had colds—and this old friend of his has bought a new cabin and he's been asking us—"

Katie Rose broke in, "I'm sorry, Mrs. Purdum, but I've already promised Mrs. McHarg to stay with their little girls." She didn't mention that she wasn't due there until four-thirty.

Stacy was suddenly clutching Katie Rose's elbow and saying, "Hey, tell her I'll come."

Katie Rose covered the phone with her palm and said in a dire whisper, "It's Mrs. Purdum."

"I know. But they've got a basket tacked onto their garage, and I can practice shooting. Ask her when she wants me."

Mrs. Purdum would like a baby-sitter just as soon as she could get there.

Ben and Mother offered to drop Stacy off on their way to the salvage yards. She hunted and found her own basketball. "I don't think the Purdum kids have a regulation ball. That's why I'm taking mine."

"Better take a baseball bat to use on those little hellions," Ben advised as they set out.

Katie Rose fell to sprucing up the house. Surely it wouldn't take Bruce long to run a visitor out to the airport. Again the brazen white enamel fixtures sat in the hall with Leo back in Bannon for the weekend. (His progress had been somewhat hampered by a running feud with the plumbing inspector.)

Ben's strength was not at hand to move the offending fixtures, and neither were the littles within shouting distance. Katie Rose herself tugged and tussled them inch by inch across the hall floor and out of sight in the bathroom.

Her arms still ached when she took a bath upstairs.

She put on her frilly, swirly, coral-colored dress. It was a little dressy for a Saturday afternoon at home, but, after all, on such a beautiful day when all the doors and windows were open, a person felt like something gay and summery.

Jeanie telephoned, all agog with plans. The John-Toms wanted to know if they couldn't take the girls over to the kite-flying contest at the park. "Let's phone Miguel too. We can get you to the McHargs' by four-thirty."

Katie Rose began enumerating household tasks she had to do, and Jeanie broke in with, "Is Bruce coming down? Is that why all the hemming and hawing?"

But she wouldn't have to hem and haw if Jeanie weren't so unsympathetic about her altruism in helping out a fellow student who was behind in lit. "He said he might come," Katie Rose admitted.

Jeanie's voice was slightly rancid, "It doesn't pay to sit at home and wait for any boy who *might* come, goose girl."

Two-thirty. Three.

Miguel stopped in. He checked on the headway Leo had made. He told Katie Rose she looked pretty in her petunia dress. He had his grandfather's car. "I'm going to the library to get him some books to read. I thought maybe somebody would need to be taken someplace."

"Nobody needs to go anyplace," she said uneasily. "Stacy's baby-sitting—if you want to call it that. She went to the Purdums' so she could practice shooting baskets."

"Yes, I know. I passed there on my way over." He studied her again, noting perhaps that her cheeks were flushed the same rosy coral as her dress; noting perhaps that she kept glancing at the clock. He asked bluntly, "Are you expecting Bruce?"

"Well, you see he still hasn't turned in anything on *Hiawatha*," she evaded, "and you know it is sort of hard to—"

"Did he *tell* you he'd be over?"

Her voice was snappish, "He said he *might* have to take some friend of his mother's to the airport—but it doesn't take long to drive out there."

He hesitated as though he didn't know whether to say something or to keep quiet. After a long pause, he asked, "Do you want a ride to the McHargs'?"

He had often taken her there. The McHarg parents, as well as the little girls, were very fond of him. Again Katie Rose turned vague. Mr. McHarg usually picked her up, she said. But she didn't tell Miguel that she had told Mrs. McHarg this morning he needn't bother—she would get there on her own. When Miguel left she stole a glance at the clock. There was still time for Bruce to arrive, drink a coke, and talk about

Hiawatha, and then drive her the few blocks to her baby-sitting job.

Bruce hadn't come when the phone rang at four. She heard the clink of coins which meant it was a toll call. It was Mrs. Purdum. Their friends in the mountains just insisted on their staying and having a steak supper with them— "They want to barbecue it on their new grill—but the evenings get so cold up here, so I'll bet anything we'll have to eat it inside—and I've been *calling* and *calling* at home to get Stacy to ask her if she could stay on with the children, and I'm just so worried because no one answers—and I can't imagine why no one—"

"They're probably all outside playing basketball, Mrs. Purdum."

"Oh, do you think so? Oh dear, I hope Lennie keeps his shoes on. Oh *dear,* Katie Rose, I'm calling from a pay phone in a filling station down the canyon—but if nobody answers at home, how am I going to—?"

"I can tell her," Katie Rose offered. "I can go past and—"

"Tell her to scramble eggs for their supper—I think there're enough—and tell her not to let Chucky eat a lot of graham crackers because if he does he won't eat his egg—coddled for him because he's only a year—and she can make toast, only the pop-up toaster doesn't pop up—you have to reach in with a fork and pull it out. Tell her the peanut butter is in the automatic washer—if I don't hide it they scoop it out with their fingers. And when they go to bed, it's Lennie's turn to take the pink panda. We'll be back early—it won't be later than nine—"

Katie Rose hung up, thankful that poor Stacy, and not she, was stuck with feeding and bedding down the four Purdums.

She left a message on the slate they called the idiot board that Stacy was staying on at the Purdums'. Bruce or no Bruce, she must set out for the McHargs' some eight blocks away. She could pass the Purdums' en route.

She threw a sweater over her sleeveless dress and went down the front steps into the sunny afternoon. She still hoped to meet Bruce on the way. Or he might show up at the McHargs'. She had taken pains to tell him where she was baby-sitting this evening, and that the McHargs never objected to a friend stopping in to keep her company.

The Purdum house, white clapboard with green trim, sat on the corner. It had been built, as Katie Rose knew, the same time as the other houses in the neighborhood. But by now it looked more scuffed and hard-used than its neighbors; one shutter was awry, a gutter hung loose, and a legless teddy bear lay bleaching on the low garage roof.

Before Katie Rose came in full view of the basket fastened onto the garage, she knew from the noisy shouts of the young Purdums and the thump of a basketball where she would find Stacy and her wards.

She stopped across the street. She had walked fast and she stood by the side of a hedge and looked toward the scene of basketball activity. She saw a lot of things that registered but dimly in her mind—the basket nailed onto the peeling green garage doors, the three Purdums bouncing about on the ground, plus the youngest in a stroller, but also bouncing up and down and adding to the din. Their beagle named Winnie contributed a yelp or two. All centered around Stacy, the star performer.

But Katie Rose's eyes did not rest on her while they widened, while they stared in shock and disbelief. They were on the boy with his close-cropped dark curly hair, on the broad shoulders filling out a beautiful, creamy-white, lumpy sweater. He must have picked it up at the cleaner's, part of her mind thought.

She stood rooted to the spot, unconsciously shrinking back into the prickly hedge behind her. Yet she needn't have worried about being seen. Stacy had eyes only for the ball which the vying Purdums caught and threw back to her, and then eyes only for the basket. Bruce Seerie had eyes only for Stacy. Once he checked her throwing to give her some instructions to which she listened raptly. She changed her stance and her grip on the ball.

Bruce shook his head. He reached his arms around and over her shoulders. He put his hands over hers and made a round, twirling motion.

Katie Rose's lips curled. That was putting on a little English, no doubt.

Stacy threw and made a basket. She threw it again and again. Each time, it went through the hoop, was delayed a small second by the net before it fell with a soft thump to the cement below. Each time, the eager Purdums ran to retrieve it for her. Each time, she looked down to see if she were standing on the chalk mark Bruce must have measured off for her. She tossed the ball the fourth time; it, too, dropped in the basket and slurped through the net.

"Four in a row, Bruce—four in a row!" You could have heard her delighted scream two blocks away. Yes, and the Purdum tribe echoing it. Her instructor grabbed her by the elbows, shouting something like, "You can't miss—you can't miss!" and in his exuberance, he picked her up by the elbows and lifted her off the ground.

That would have been enough for the amazed watcher across the street. But Stacy, as he lifted her higher, lost her equilibrium—or did she just pretend to?—and doubled over so that her head with its fanning red hair was brushing his cheek, and her feet were flailing, and she was laughing with him and crying out, "Bruce, Bruce—I'm falling—" And those loudmouth Purdums screeching like Indians.

Of course Stacy didn't fall. Of course Bruce let her down. But he steadied her by holding her close while they laughed on in joyous abandon. Katie Rose had to turn her eyes away. He had never been like that with her. He had never looked at her as if—as if he wanted to kiss her.

She stood there, not feeling the leafless hedge pricking through her sweater and into her back. What could she do now? She couldn't be the *outsider* walking in and disrupting such—such intimacy. Couldn't she just skirt around the hedge and go on to the McHargs', and let Stacy and Bruce and the Purdums fight it out together?

But before she could take a step, the oldest Purdum saw her and shouted across to her, "Katie Rose, whatta you know? She made four in a row—four in a row!"

Bruce and Stacy backed away from each other and watched her as she crossed the street. Well, she was certainly as welcome as Banquo's ghost at the banquet! She said—and she meant it to sound very casual but it came out cold and reproving, "Mrs. Purdum tried and tried to phone you from the mountains, and she couldn't imagine why there was no answer."

Stacy, breathing hard from her exertion, panted out, "I told her I was going to practice."

Bruce was now dribbling the ball on the cement apron of the garage. He said, without looking at the newcomer, "First she was only making two out of four. Then she got up to three out of four, and just now she made four baskets in four shots."

"I saw her." Did they expect her to jump up and down and shout Hallelujah? She added, "Stacy, the Purdums are staying up in the mountains till nine, and they want you to stay. She said for you to scramble eggs for supper, and not to let Chucky stuff himself on graham crackers." She glanced at the baby in his stroller and saw that the injunction had come too late. His hands and face, as well as his outer garment called a cuddle bunny, were well smeared with them, and a border of broken pieces surrounded the stroller. Winnie's disappointed sniffs at them were proof that she was not a graham cracker addict. "And then you're to put them to bed."

One of the Purdums bellowed, "My turn—my turn to have the pink panda."

"It's Lennie's, your mother said. And she said to make toast, only the toaster doesn't pop up."

Stacy still stood, out of breath and her face flushed

and moist. She pulled the rubber band off her hair, and shook the reddish blond disarray vigorously. Using her fingers as a comb, she swooped it up into a neater pony tail and tightened the band around it. She said blithely, "Oh, we'll manage all right. Are you on your way to McHargs'?"

Bruce looked at her for the first time, and said heartily, "I'll run you over, Katie Rose. I've got the car."

She bent her head in sudden panic, feeling the sting of tears behind her eyes, and a lump—it seemed as big as the basketball he was holding—in her throat. She turned away and said airily over her shoulder, "Oh no—no, thanks, it's just a step—I'll be there before you could start the car."

She made herself saunter, not run. She must hold to the "I couldn't care less" attitude. No tear must fall until she was out of sight. She had gone only a block when she saw ahead the two little McHarg girls, Diane and Debbie, in front of their house waiting for her. They came running to meet her. Was there no privacy in her unprivate world? They each took one of her hands and, chattering like magpies, escorted her on to their house and through their front door.

The McHarg residence, inside and out, was as ordered as the Purdums' was disordered. The McHarg modern equipment always worked to perfection. You'd never find a pop-up toaster there refusing to pop up. So were the two little blond girls beautifully disciplined and mannered. You'd never catch one of them scooping peanut butter out of the jar with her fingers.

Heavens, Katie Rose had forgotten to tell Stacy the hiding place of the peanut butter. Well, they could go peanut butterless for all of her.

The smooth-running McHarg home was not only a contrast to the Purdums' but to the Belfords' as well. Katie Rose was always quoting Mrs. McHarg and her efficiency to her mother. Sometimes her mother teased back, "So she runs herself and her house by the clock, does she? Does she set the timer when she drinks a cup of coffee?"

"She's not a fanatic about her routine," Katie Rose would say. "But she keeps abreast of her work. She wouldn't have ironing—say for—"

"Let me *say*," her mother laughed. "For three years now I've never seen the bottom of the clothes-basket. And if I don't for another three, I'll be losing no sleep over it."

But sometimes Mother's mood would not be receptive to McHarg perfections; especially when they sat down to tea and found they were out of sugar, or when she started a washing and found the box of detergent empty. "So your woman has revolving cupboard shelves and knows what she has and what she hasn't! Now isn't that ducky? And if I had only two meek and mild little angels and nothing else to do—"

About then Ben would say, "That's enough Mc-Harg, Katie Rose. Mom's got a wooden spoon in her hand, and a swatting gleam in her eye."

But Katie Rose was secretly convinced that when she married, she would run a shining house with the same smooth skill as Mrs. McHarg.

This late afternoon she was already dressed for a golf celebration at the club with her husband, and she greeted Katie Rose warmly. "I'm always so happy to have you here, Katie Rose."

"I'm always happy to be here."

But it was hard for her to concentrate on Mrs. McHarg's instructions. "Here are the avocado halves in the refrigerator—I rubbed them with lemon juice to keep them from discoloring. And here's the chicken salad to fill them with. I thought as long as we were going to a party, you could make a party out of your dinner here too. Maybe you'd like to ask your date—that nice Miguel."

Her big, genial, golf-playing husband called out from the living room, "We know a pretty gal like you would be having a Saturday night date if you weren't helping us out." And the little girls entreated, "Yes, Katie Rose, ask Miguel."

She suspected the older McHargs of liking him because he was the son of a prominent writer. Diane and Debbie loved him because he was Miguel and could wiggle his ears and tell them hair-raising stories.

"He's out someplace. He's pretty busy helping— you see, his grandfather's knee is in a cast." This was certainly her afternoon of evasions. But she didn't want to see Miguel. He *knew*. Only an hour ago when she had told him Stacy was at the Purdums', he had said, "Yes, I know. I drove past there." That's why he had asked, "Are you expecting Bruce?" and "Did he *tell* you he was coming?"

She didn't want to see anyone. She wanted to keep saying to herself, "I couldn't care less."

The McHarg parents said their good-bys. Katie Rose watched them walk out to their car and thought, It must be wonderful to be old and comfortable and not have a care in the world.

She filled the avocado halves with chicken salad, and took the scalloped potatoes out of the oven. She said gaily, "Isn't this fun? We'll have a party all by ourselves." But she forgot to light the candles on the glass-topped table until the little girls reminded her. White candles in squat blue holders of Mexican glass. The pitcher Diane poured chocolate milk from, and the glasses she poured it into, were also blue Mexican glass.

Diane and Debbie put on their frilly and abbreviated pajamas, blue for Diane, pink for Debbie. They pulled on their blue and pink quilted robes. Diane said, "Mother said we could stay up till *eight* tonight, so you could tell us all about everything you're doing at school."

"We're putting on a school play next month."

"Our cousin goes to high school, and they had their play last month," they told her.

"We're late at Adams," she said absently. "We've been late with everything because it's a new school. They have to do something about acoustics in the auditorium during spring vacation."

"Are you going to be in the play, Katie Rose?"

"I'm sure I will. I tried out for it."

"What did you do when you tryouted?"

"I danced and sang to 'I Could Dance All Night.' "

"Please, Katie Rose, dance for us and sing for us what you did."

She went through it for her admiring audience of two. She relived that tryout in the empty auditorium even to her coming down the steps and seeing Mrs. Dujardin's complimentary smile. She hugged her words close to her heart, "Very good, child, very good. You have that same quality Zoe has of getting across to the audience." Katie Rose hugged Howard's praise close too, "Aren't you the one!—breaking into that slip-slap step to waltz time."

"And after you danced and sang, what did you do?"

"I took the part of Ophelia."

"Who's Ophelia?"

"She was a girl who loved Hamlet, and she thought —she thought he loved her—"

"Do that for us too, Katie Rose," they begged.

"Her father's name was Polonius, and he said to Ophelia, 'What is between you? Give me up the truth.' And poor—*dumb* little Ophelia said, 'He hath, my lord, of late made many tenders of his affection toward me.' That meant that he had made her think that he—he was crazy about her."

"What'd her father say when she said that?"

"He said, 'Affection! Pooh! You have taken these tenders for true pay which are not sterling. Tender yourself more dearly.' "

"What'd that mean?"

"That meant that Ophelia thought it was the real thing when all the time Hamlet didn't care—he didn't care a hoot about her."

"She *was* dumb, wasn't she, Katie Rose?"

"Yes, she was." And so had Katie Rose been dumb. Building hopes on Bruce's need of her, and feeling so sure of his undying gratitude. But why not? The hours and effort she had given him—even slighting her own work to read that dull old *Hiawatha* and underline pithy passages for him . . . She winced as she pictured again that joyous intimacy beneath the Purdums' basket—his whirling Stacy off her feet, her falling hair brushing his face—his steadying her and *adoring* her—

And standing there in the McHarg living room, a passionate longing swept over Katie Rose like a tidal wave. She had to have a part in the show. That was the only thing that would ease this hurt. That would bolster up her wounded ego. That would keep her from feeling rejected and jilted. That would show Bruce and Stacy, and everyone at Adams High—yes, everyone in her world—that she was *somebody*.

II

It was like the McHargs to get home at exactly ten-fifteen after saying they would. And like the Purdums to come home around midnight when Mrs. Purdum had been sure they would be home by nine.

So Katie Rose lay awake in the double bed she shared with Stacy, and waited for her return. What would Stacy's attitude be? Contrite? Defiant? Katie Rose clamped her jaws tight. She would not give Stacy, and certainly not Bruce, the satisfaction of knowing that the pain under her ribs was like a physical ache.

But by the time Stacy tiptoed up the stairs, Katie Rose was asleep.

Every Sunday morning, Katie Rose, Ben, and Stacy sang in the choir at St. Jude's nine-thirty Mass while

Mother played the organ. The family was having a hurried cup of coffee to stay them until their return, when Stacy, heavy-eyed and tousled and clutching her robe about her, came as far down the stairs as the landing.

"Do I have to go to church and sing?" she pleaded. "I'm sore all over from shooting baskets yesterday. I can't even lift my arms."

"You don't sing with your arms," Ben said. "Get into your clothes fast."

Mother was a shade more sympathetic. "You can't take time now, but when you come back from church you can soak in a hot tub. And don't we have some of that brown linament, Katie Rose?"

"I wouldn't know," was the unconcerned answer.

They were back from Mass and going through the side gate when Stacy reproached her. "Why did you keep moving away from me up in the choir, Katie Rose, when I needed to look at your book?"

Alas for Katie Rose's I-couldn't-care-less role. She blurted out, "Because I don't like a snake in the grass, that's why."

Stacy stopped short. "Oh, for the love of Pete. Bruce just happened to be driving past, and he saw me practicing and so he stopped to coach me."

"And I suppose he just *happened* to stay the rest of the evening with you," Katie Rose sneered. Even as she did, she yearned to hear Stacy say, "He didn't stay. He left right after you were there."

"Not all evening because his folks still have him grounded. Lordy, I was ready to drop by suppertime, and all those little hyenas—one wanting this and another that, and climbing all over the cupboards, and we could only find two eggs in the icebox—"

Katie Rose's curiosity overcame her injured feelings. "Did you find the peanut butter? Mrs. Purdum said she hid it."

"Hid it, my eye! The kids knew where it was. Did you know that graham cracker drool hardens just like plaster? Honestly, the baby's zipper was simply cemented shut, and Bruce had to get his pliers out of the car—and we all had to hold the little kid down." Stacy's ready giggle spilled over.

Katie Rose walked away before she heard more. The hurt was deeper. Not that it was particularly romantic to picture Bruce and Stacy dividing two eggs among the hungry, clamoring Purdums, and prying the youngest out of his cuddle bunny, but it was the very closeness, the oneness of them that stabbed.

It was almost too much to bear alone. But who could she tell, "Stacy took my boy friend from me"? Not Mom; certainly not Ben. Jeanie? She would have every right to say, "I told you so." But Katie Rose was in such dire need of telling someone that she phoned

her, saying aloud to anyone within hearing, "I just
envy Jeanie having a phone extension in her own
room."

She had no sooner said hello, than Jeanie answered,
"Wait till I switch the phone to my other ear," and
then, "My doggone' Eustachian tube is acting up
again and I can't hear out of that one."

"Oh, that's too bad. Are you in your own room?"

"Yes, with Dad dosing me up and, at the moment,
shaking down a thermometer."

"Oh." She had thought of inviting herself to Jeanie's just to pour out her woe. But not with Jeanie's
doctor father hovering close. She said in a forlorn
voice, "I'll wait then and tell you what I was going to
tell you at school tomorrow."

"On the weathercast it said our halcyon days are
over. But, as I tell Dad, I've got red earmuffs Ben
presented to me. If I don't make it, would you bring
me the lesson assignments? It's quite a trek if it's
stormy, but ask Ben to bring you. I'd like to see him
too."

Katie Rose lowered her voice to a mumble, "I
couldn't tell you about—I couldn't tell you in front
of Ben."

A pause. "Is it Bruce?"

"Uh-huh."

"Well, if Ben comes I'll ask him to go get some ice

cream or something, and then you can tell me. I'm sorry I can't talk any more now, but this man in my life is about to chuck a thermometer in my mouth."

The weatherman had predicted truly. The next day the sky was a gunmetal gray and the air brooding and chill.

Jeanie Kincaid was not at school.

Katie Rose left third-hour math with only one idea —to avoid Bruce. For the past two weeks he had met her at the drinking fountain and walked with her to Madame Miller's French. Ah, the bright and beautiful spot that had been in her day.

This morning she scurried past the fountain without stopping, and made for the stairs. She saw him coming up before he saw her. He was carrying his head high and swinging his shoulders as though the world were his for the asking. Until he saw her, that is. He stammered an embarrassed, "Well hi, Katie Rose."

"Hi, Bruce." She would have hurried past him on the stairs, but he stopped in front of her. "Listen— about Saturday. You see, I'd been to the airport, and I was driving by and I saw Stacy shooting baskets. And I just figured that maybe I could help her get the hang of—"

"Oh sure, Bruce. That's all right." Again hope

pushed into her being. Maybe he'd say, "I wanted to help her because she's your young sister, and it seemed little enough after all you've done for me." And couldn't a fellow have gotten so carried away by having such an apt pupil that he picked her up and whirled her—?

"Gee, Katie Rose, I'm glad you're not—I mean I'm glad you don't mind." His brown eyes turned bemused and smiling. "I've never known anyone like her before. I mean, she's so real. She never tries to impress you. And I—I like the way she gets such a kick out of life—you know, when she cries, she cries all over, and when she laughs—"

Katie Rose's laugh was forced and ragged. "I know. Stacy hasn't an inhibition in the world."

"That's right. And that's what's so—so different about her. Katie Rose, it isn't that I don't appreciate your trying to help me—" He was fumbling for words.

Her *trying* to help him! His other fumbled words had been so many knife thrusts, but that was twisting the knife in the wound. As though she hadn't limbered up his wooden report on *The Old Man and—* and wised him up on *Hamlet*—not to mention steering him onto Walt Whitman. Not to mention her own hard going on *Hiawatha* which they would never discuss now.

For he was giving her the go-by. Numbed as she was, she must hang on to her pride. It was a poor cloak, but it was all she had. She said, "I won't have a bit of extra time now. Any day Mrs. Dujardin will give out parts for the musical comedy, and we won't have much time for learning parts and rehearsals — No, I won't have a minute to waste on trying to help anybody."

He needn't think he'd have her around his neck!

The bell rang, and she had time only to see the surprised and baffled look on his face before she turned and raced down the stairs to French.

At noon when Katie Rose reached in her locker for her sack of lunch, Deetsy asked, "And how's the lady tutor and her handsome scholar getting along?"

Walkie-talkie Deetsy! Know-it-all Deetsy! It won't be long, Katie Rose thought, before she finds out that the lady tutor is out, and her young sister is in. And what Deetsy knew the whole school would know.

Katie Rose answered with a blithe shrug, "The handsome scholar is a little thick in the head."

If only Mrs. Dujardin would give out the parts! Then Katie Rose could proclaim to the world that she had no time for helping Bruce. She could even intimate that he had taken up with Stacy as second choice.

She suddenly had no heart for facing the luncheon group. June would be sitting there, eating the hearty plate lunch that never put an ounce on her, and wearing her Mona Lisa smile because her affairs of the heart always went off well. Deetsy would be prattling about heaven knows what. The John-Toms would scold her for not going to the park with them Saturday afternoon. (She'd have been better off to watch the kite-flying.) The nice, polite, and untalkative George would look at her with X-ray eyes that seemed to read her thoughts.

And Miguel. Miguel knew that while she waited at home in her petunia dress, Bruce was having himself a time with a girl who cried all over and laughed all over, and who happened to be Katie Rose's sister.

She took only an apple tart out of her sack of lunch, and went to the sewing room. Girls often worked there through their noon hour. She ate her tart, and struggled halfheartedly with the zipper in the rose denim skirt she was making until the fifth-hour bell rang.

Mr. Jacoby stood in his study hall door while pupils filed in and took their seats. A glance inside told Katie Rose that Miguel had no sun to measure today, but only a misted-over window he couldn't see through.

Mrs. Dujardin was walking down the hall. Feeling a

driving need, she asked Mr. Jacoby if he could excuse her a few minutes to talk to her.

He nodded agreeably, and asked, "How are you doing on your autobiography, Kathleen?"

"I'm giving it a lot of thought."

"Give it a lot of *you*. I'm looking forward to your turning in something worthwhile. Remember to mention important milestones."

Ah yes, milestones!

She caught up with Mrs. Dujardin as she went in the door that led to the greenroom behind the auditorium stage. The drama teacher seemed not to have wholly recovered her lively vigor after her illness. Her black eyes lacked their usual sparkle and, as she halted, she pulled the black sweater more snugly over her shoulders.

Katie Rose said, "I just wondered if you'd decided over the weekend on the musical comedy we—you—will be putting on."

"Not yet, dear. I'll bet I've read twenty in the last two days. The problem is to find one to fit our drama talent, and yet with a musical score that isn't too difficult for the orchestra to handle."

Say it, please say it, Mrs. Du. "But you'll have a part in whichever we select, Katie Rose."

Howard, who was always at hand to help, called to

her from the stage, "I got the two tenors for you to listen to, Mrs. Dujardin. Mr. Hill will be right back. He ducked out for coffee."

But Katie Rose had to impress on Mrs. Dujardin that she was no rank amateur who might get stage fright and lose her voice in front of an audience. "I guess you might say, acting runs in our family. Grandda—I mean my Grandfather O'Byrne—was with the Abbey players in Dublin from the time he was fifteen until he left there and came to Bannon, and he—"

"Do you mean Urban O'Byrne? And he's your grandfather? I know him. When I was in teachers' college years ago, he came over from Bannon and helped our drama coach cast and direct our play. Yes, I remember him well." Her eyes still on Katie Rose's eager face, she added slowly, "I've never forgotten his telling us about the Abbey system of casting." A pause. "By the way, don't you have study hall this period?"

"Mr. Jacoby excused me for a few minutes." She went on swiftly, "Summer before last when Grandda was directing *Philadelphia Story* for the Tri-county Players, the girl who was playing the younger sister Dinah got hurt from a horse stepping on her foot— and you know what a bouncy part Dinah is—so

Grandda came in and took me out to Bannon and drilled me in the part. I only had two weeks—and you know what a long part Dinah has—and I never fumbled a word. Grandda says I'm a quick study."

She paused for breath. *Say what you said to Zoe about counting on my talent. Say it, so I can go back to study hall with something to hold to.*

Mrs. Dujardin only surveyed her silently. Mr. Hill was coming toward them with a cup of coffee. The woman took it with a grateful, "Thank you, Pete." Then, "You'd better get back to study hall, Katie Rose."

A misty rain was falling when school closed. Katie Rose stood at her locker and watched students halting at the quadruple glass doors to grope for parka hoods and pull them over their heads.

Now where was Ben to drive her to Jeanie's?

Whenever she wanted him, she always looked first in biology lab. He was there this gloomy afternoon with his working partner, Grace. (Yes, someone ought to tell Grace that yellow wasn't her shade when her skin had a sallow tinge.)

Katie Rose stood in the doorway, hoping Ben would see her and come over. She didn't want to walk up to him *and* Grace, who was forever phoning him about thoraxes and tympanums, and say, "You're to take me to Jeanie's, remember? She said she'd like to see you."

Neither of them looked her way. Their whole attention was on a small, dark object lying on a paper towel on the table, which they were turning over gently and lovingly. Other students were in the lab; two boys at a far table, and a girl writing in her notebook. But they were relaxed and visiting together. They were not the dedicated scientists Ben and Grace were.

Katie Rose approached them. "What is that—a dead bee?"

They both raised absorbed eyes, and Grace answered, "A *queen* bee. Isn't she beautiful?"

"Ben, I promised to take Jeanie her lesson assignments, and it's raining."

"Oh, is it raining?" he said in a faraway voice. "We've just got the bee for a while to make drawings." And Grace put in in a breathless voice, "We want to make them with crayon, so we can show her red stinger and incandescent wings."

Katie Rose stood a minute longer, hoping Grace might leave to get a notebook or red pencil so she could say, "Ben, Jeanie's expecting you."

Instead Grace bent over the fuzzy object, murmuring, "Oughtn't we to straighten out this one leg, Ben?"

His whole attention and a carefully probing forefinger were given over to that.

There was nothing for Katie Rose to do but walk out of the lab and leave them to their beautiful bee.

After leaving Adams
High and walking some ten winding Harmony
Heights blocks through the mizzling rain, Katie Rose
knocked on the Kincaid pink door. Jeanie's tall,
blond, and usually serene mother opened it.

She was not quite so serene today. "Katie Rose, you
walked through the rain! Come on in the kitchen a
minute—and here, let me take your wet jacket.
Wouldn't you know that on a rainy day like this our
clothes dryer would decide to have tantrums."

Over the ominous clickety-clack of the dryer, and
Mrs. Kincaid running water in a small vase, Jeanie
called out from the living room, "Come on in here,
Katie Rose." The phone in the kitchen pealed, and
Mrs. Kincaid had time only to flick off the dryer with
a grimace and a muttered, "Sounds like it's working

up to an explosion," and to motion to the vase with, "Take it in with you, honey," before she lifted the receiver.

Jeanie got up from the living room couch to greet Katie Rose. In her short red corduroy peignoir, with her tumbled brown hair caught back with combs, and no lipstick on, Jeanie looked very childlike and small.

Another caller was already there. It was the boy who always walked from journalism to her locker with Jeanie; the one she called Robert Burns while he called her Highland Mary. He, too, must have just arrived, for his hair and shoes were still wet, and he was holding three daffodils in his hand.

Katie Rose took them and fitted them into the vase. "I didn't know any daffodils were out yet."

"These were growing under a little bridge, and nobody told them it wasn't April yet," he answered.

Jeanie giggled. "He's crazy, Katie Rose. Last summer he got a job herding sheep in Montana, thirty-two miles from even a mailbox, just so he could commune with nature."

"And the sheep," he added gravely. "They set me right on a lot of misleading information. White sheep are a dirty white, and black sheep aren't really black —they're dingy brown. Lambs aren't meek and mild either. They just pretend to be so people will carve them on tombstones. Once I had to catch a little fellow and hand-feed him, and he kicked me right in the eye."

Mrs. Kincaid came into the room. "That was Dad on the phone, Jeanie. He wants me to drive down and pick him up at the hospital." She smiled apologetically at Robert Burns. "I'm sorry to give you the bum's .rush, but the doctor's orders are to get Jeanie to bed and put drops in her ear."

"Pity the doctor's poor daughter," Jeanie said.

Robert Burns got leisurely to his feet—you couldn't imagine his ever hurrying. He reached over and righted one of his daffodils in the vase, and picked up his jacket from the couch arm.

"It's still wet," Jeanie said, with regret in her voice.

He turned his slow, absent smile on them as he started for the door. "I read a Japanese poem once. It was written as though a fisherman wrote it, and it was something like this: 'The sleeve of my jacket is wet— but not as wet as my cheek from tears.' I've always wondered why his cheek was wet from tears." He didn't bother with conventional good-bys but with a fond smile for them all—especially Jeanie—he ambled toward the door Mrs. Kincaid opened for him. "The rain is making up its mind to be snow," he imparted.

Jeanie's mother closed the door gently after him, shaking her head as she did. "I hope he doesn't roam around in the rain talking to daffodils. You stay, Katie Rose, and keep Jeanie company. But march her into bed while I warm the oil for the drops."

Jeanie stood up. "We're on our way."

It was easy for Katie Rose to envy Jeanie this "room of her own" with its Scotch plaid draperies and spread, her study table and book shelves, the hi-fi set, *and* phone extension. Today the room had a pungent steaminess from the vaporizer on the bedside table.

Jeanie sat on the bed and kicked off her red, fuzzy scuffies. "I hope you won't be overpowered by the eucalyptus oil smell, Katie Rose. Isn't Robert Burns a lovable goon?"

She said it so fondly and looked so pleased with life, and so unconcerned about Katie Rose's problems, that Katie Rose found herself saying, "Ben wouldn't bring me. He and his lab partner were too enraptured over a queen bee with a red stinger."

She was ashamed the minute she said it, for Jeanie suddenly looked like a girl who had stayed out of school because she was sick.

"I know," Jeanie nodded. "Not only enraptured but so *en rapport*. Now it's the bee. Last week when Ben took me to the Robin for a hamburger, it was the grasshopper."

Before Katie Rose could explain that she had only spoken out of her own misery, Jeanie's mother came into the room. She had already put on a transparent raincoat, and was carrying a medicine dropper as though it were a small torch. She bent over the recumbent Jeanie, and the drops went in her ear.

"Keep your little noggin flat on the pillow for at least five minutes," her mother admonished. "I have to hurry off. I left a pan of cocoa on the stove for you—it only needs to be warmed up."

"Fine, Mom. Maybe we can drown our sorrows in cocoa."

Mrs. Kincaid turned at the doorway. "You've got sorrows! I've got a dryer on the fritz. If you feel up to it, Jeanie, could you fish out a couple of Dad's white shirts and, if the dryer didn't dry them, hang them on a register to finish."

"I'll do it," Katie Rose volunteered.

"We'll both do it," Jeanie said from her pillow. "So get going, Mom. You know how the doctor hates to be kept waiting."

The door had no sooner closed behind her than Jeanie asked, "What did Bruce do or didn't do, Katie Rose?"

"He gave me the go-by for Stacy," she said bluntly.

"Stacy? You're kidding. Of course, Stacy is all sparkle and shine, and I never saw her skating at the park that she wasn't completely surrounded by boys. But Bruce is so—so not the kind to go overboard."

"That's what you think."

Katie Rose told the whole story, mentioning again the fight at St. Jude's, and Bruce's great interest in Stacy's basket shooting. She made it factual, even to Bruce's not committing himself to coming to Hubbell Street Saturday afternoon. She ended with her watching Bruce's coaching Stacy in the Purdum yard, and their joyous hilarity, and their clinging to each other. "You know, there's that certain way a boy looks at a girl when he's far gone on—"

Jeanie broke in, "Are you sure you're not imagining it? Sure he isn't just trying to bring up her scoring —as one basketball forward to another?"

Katie Rose's lips crimped. "I—I kept hoping maybe that was it. But this morning— You should have heard him. He's never known anyone like Stacy—she laughs all over and cries all over. She's so real—so everything—he's ever dreamed of. She's his Miss Irresistible."

She paused and waited for Jeanie to say indignantly that it was a crummy way for a boy to treat a girl who had given her all to bring him up in lit. (Wading through that boring jumble of *Hiawatha* when she didn't have to!) But Jeanie only pulled herself up on the pillow, holding a paper tissue to her ear, and stared thoughtfully at Katie Rose on the foot of the bed while the vapor kettle burbled on.

Katie Rose prodded, "Here's your chance for a big, fat I-told-you-so. Or don't you remember telling me he was wrong for me and I was wrong for him? And you're so right. He's a different person since the ravishing Stacy came into his life."

Jeanie didn't say I-told-you-so. Her voice was almost a moan, "Oh, goose girl, if only you could see Bruce as I see him—as he really is. Just a well-mannered athlete, a bit mother-ridden, who had to wear braces on his out-jutting teeth to get that beautiful smile you're always talking about. If only you didn't put him on a pedestal with a rose-colored aura—"

Katie Rose hurled back, "Okay, and I can't see anything poetic or Robert Burnsy about this fellow you think is so lovable." Again she wanted to hurt or anger Jeanie. "He's just a sawed-off little runt to me."

Jeanie only laughed. "I know, and with a flat head to boot. You're right, Robert Burns wouldn't seem like much to you, but there's something about him—" She broke off, and added musingly, "The only good thing about having a bum Eustachian tube is that you can lie here and think—I guess 'meditate' is the word. And I keep thinking of Miguel and his saying once that the heart has a lot of rooms. And that's because the heart has a lot of different needs—"

"*Thus Spake Zarathustra*," Katie Rose mocked. It was comfort she wanted, not philosophy.

Unheeding, Jeanie went on. "And maybe it's because my folks are so practical that part of me is thrilled to the core when Robert Burns brings me a few lopsided daffodils. He calls me Highland Mary and right away I feel so sort of 'lissome' and 'down the rushy glen.' And Ben. The clinging vine side of me likes his strength and bossiness—"

"He's crazy about you. I just made that crack about him and Grace because—well, I guess it's true that misery loves company."

"I'm jealous of her," Jeanie admitted, "even though I realize he'd rather dance with me and have fun with me. Even though I can understand how one side of him—"

"Rooms. You started out with rooms, Jeanie."

"So I did. Well then, another room in Ben's heart is filled by Grace's sharing his passionate interest in grass-hoppers and bees. And I've got a room in my heart where I want to be a columnist, and there's where I've got the editor-in-chief of our paper. The day he even notices me is a red-letter day. But Mr. Knight is right about this being a getting-to-know-you time. And it's even a getting-to-know-yourself time."

"I suppose all this is leading up to your telling me to put Bruce back in the storeroom again?"

Jeanie looked at her with love and sympathy. She said abruptly, "Let's heat up the cocoa while I fish out Dad's shirts. If they're dry enough I might even iron one, because Mom has had quite a day of it. They're the drip-dry kind that don't need much."

They were just right to iron, and while Jeanie heated the cocoa, Katie Rose ironed two. "These are a joy to whisk over," she said, "after ironing those stiff old jackets of Ben's."

"You're a love, Katie Rose." Jeanie set the mugs of cocoa on the narrow bar between the kitchen and dining area, and pulled up stools. "Now drink your cocoa because what I'm going to say will be hard for you to take."

"I know—the storeroom for Bruce."

"No storeroom this time. The back door. And slam it hard. But this is what you won't like. I can see Bruce's side in all this too. Now wait—wait," Jeanie scolded, as Katie Rose choked and sputtered on her swallow of cocoa. "Try and put yourself in his shoes. Here he was, feeling so bottom of the barrel from being kicked off the team. Okay, so there you were right at hand to be his literary savior. But all your help—and honestly, didn't you try to impress him? —didn't do a thing for his battered ego—"

"Impress him! How could I help him if I didn't know more than he did? Too bad about his battered ego!"

Jeanie ignored the outburst. "You probably worsened it because he couldn't help knowing how much smarter you are. But he could feel like a hero around Stacy. So I can understand his needing her to reach out to."

"To, and around." She meant it to be flippant but her voice cracked.

Jeanie patted her knee. "I know how it hurts, and how it seems like the end of the world."

"It wouldn't be if—if Mrs. Du would just give out the parts for the play," Katie Rose gulped.

"You're sure to get a peachy part. Mrs. Du has always bragged about you," Jeanie comforted. "And you've always got Miguel with his zombie outside and good solid core inside."

Katie Rose smiled at that. "He says that it's in the stars for either of us to go running whenever one of us is in a·jam and needs help." But even that couldn't ease the hurting lump in her middle. She asked helplessly, "What am I going to do, Jeanie?"

Jeanie refilled Katie Rose's cup, and said almost gently, "There's nothing you can do, goose girl. Except to hide your aching heart."

Katie Rose finished her cocoa. It did help in drown-

ing some of her sorrow. Talking it out with Jeanie
had helped too. Her heart felt a little lighter. She gave
Jeanie the lesson assignments, and they gossiped idly
about fellow students and teachers.

She noticed Jeanie's wan face as she righted one of
the combs in her thick, heavy hair, and said con-
tritely, "You'd better get back to bed. I'm going." She
reached for her coat.

"Yes, I'd better, before Dad gets home." But her
parting words as Katie Rose reached for the doorknob
were, "Whatever you do, Katie Rose, don't be mean
or spiteful toward Bruce and Stacy."

"Oh, I won't—not for anything. Besides, I'm beginning to feel almost as philosophical as you do about it
now."

She walked home, breathing in the damp air that
felt all the fresher after the medicated steam in Jeanie's room. By the time she reached Hubbell the drizzle,
as Robert Burns predicted, had made up its mind to
be snow. She leaned against a tree and pulled her
parka hood more snugly over her head.

Two blocks down the street she saw a cream-colored convertible pulling away from the curb in front
of the Belford house and turning east toward Harmony Heights. So Bruce had driven to St. Jude's for
Stacy and brought her home. But not *directly* home.
There had been an hour's lingering someplace.

Being philosophical about losing a boy friend to a sister was one thing, but seeing it in action was quite another. Hurt and fury churned up inside her. She had to lean against the tree for several minutes before she walked on dragging feet through the wet, sudsy snow.

She walked in the side door just as Mother was scalding out the brown earthenware teapot. "Why, you're sopping wet, child. Get into dry shoes while I brew the tea. And never mind looking to see if there's any progress in the bath. There's none. Leo didn't come in from Bannon because Grandda has to do his carpentering before he can go any further. And that picky plumbing inspector still has to inspect what Leo did over."

At least, Katie Rose thought wryly, she would no longer have to worry about those heavy fixtures being in plain sight, or have to tussle them into the closet.

As she climbed the stairs, a pungent medicinal odor grew stronger. It was different from the one at Jeanie's, and was somehow familiar and reminiscent.

The full force of it met her when she opened the door to the room she shared with Stacy. And no wonder. Stacy was disrobed of her St. Jude plaid jumper and white blouse, and Jill was rubbing a milky ointment into the back of her neck and shoulders.

"What in heaven's name is that vile-smelling stuff?"

Jill answered promptly, "It's the best thing for charley horse, Bruce told Stacy. It's what the coach at Adams has the team use."

That reminiscent smell of the Adams gym, of football players—of Bruce—was an added blow to Katie Rose.

Stacy said quickly, "Jill! Why don't you ever keep your mouth shut?"

"Why don't you teach her to lie for you?" Katie Rose sneered.

Jill looked up with bright interest. "Are you gonna fight?"

Katie Rose yanked open the closet door, and Stacy said on an uncomfortable laugh, "That's enough rubbing my shoulders, Jill. Go on down and get your tea."

The door closed behind her. Stacy addressed the top of her sister's head, for she was bent over, pulling on dry slippers, "I don't see why you're treating me like dirt, Katie Rose, just because Bruce— Listen, do you remember that I was the one who first knew Miguel? I met him at Wetzel's store, and I thought he was ginger-peachy. And what happens? He comes to the house and meets you and falls for you and starts calling you Petunia. And right away, I'm just your little sister."

"Pardon me, while I weep for you."

Stacy snapped, "Oh, stop acting like a wounded cowger."

"Do you by any chance mean *cougar?*"

Stacy didn't bother with whether it was cowger or cougar, but said, "It'd be different if you and Bruce were going steady, or you were crazy about him—"

"I AM NOT CRAZY ABOUT HIM," Katie Rose screamed. "I was just trying to help him pass lit, and now—now—" Now she hoped viciously that everything he turned in to Mr. Jacoby would be slapped right back at him.

Their mother called up the stairs, "Here's Ben. Come on, you two, before the tea gets cold."

The two walked down the stairs like utter strangers who had never met or exchanged a word.

13

The week following that Monday was an up-and-down week for Katie Rose. She had times of *almost* forgiving Stacy, of *almost* wishing Bruce well, and *almost* not feeling jilted and betrayed.

Wednesday was the seventeenth of March. Katie Rose received a St. Patrick's card from Uncle Brian in San Francisco. So did Jeanie, who often said, "I wish I had an uncle like your Uncle Brian." In sewing that morning they compared the cards, laughing in delight at the extravagant blarney on Jeanie's:

"My honey bear, my darlin' dear, I think of you every waking minute."

He wrote on Katie Rose's:

"I'm taking part in a St. Patrick skit the Lady Gregory players are putting on. Wish you were here, bright angel, to sing 'The Wearin' of the Green' with me."

"It's sweet the way he always calls you bright angel," Jeanie said. "But you were, just when he needed one, and he'll never forget it."

She was referring to a bad time when Uncle Brian gave up drinking, and Katie Rose had helped him "stay on the wagon."

"I can't wait to get a part in the school play and telephone him about it." A prayer shivered through Katie Rose.

Ever since the Belford mother had been playing the piano at Guido's Gay Nineties, Guido invited the Belford young folks out to help celebrate St. Patrick's. He always reserved a large table close to the musicians for them and for any guests they wanted to bring.

Ben arranged for his fellow-worker, Clyde, at the Ragged Robin to take his shift for him this night. He asked Jeanie to go with them. Katie Rose wasn't sure who had invited Miguel—probably everyone in the family. Stacy did *not* ask Bruce.

There was a grand furor in the Belford house that evening with everyone garbing himself suitably for the festive occasion.

Katie Rose and Stacy dressed in their Irish piper

costumes. Never before had they been so coldly polite
to each other in the process. Each had her own pleated
kilt of green handwoven wool. But only one of the
white, lace-trimmed blouses had been made in Ireland. The other was an American copy. On other
occasions, they had hotly contested which should
wear the bona fide one. But this evening, Stacy put on
the one with the dime store lace, leaving the one with
the froth of real Limerick lace for Katie Rose.

They both wore the same size shoe and Katie Rose,
not to be outdone, slid her feet into the black pumps
with the smaller silver buckles, leaving the pair with
the larger, shinier ones for Stacy. (And the bigger and
brighter the buckles, the more noticeably they twinkled through an Irish jig.)

Mother came out of her room to drape the squares
of green cloth over their shoulders and pin them in
place with heavy Tara brooches. She was wearing her
billowy green taffeta that brought out the green of
her eyes. Her St. Patrick combs, set with green stones
in the shape of shamrocks, sparkled in her red hair.

She grieved because Matt and Brian must settle for
green ties on their white shirts, and Jill with one on
her white blouse. "My own poor littles! You've been
neglected in not having costumes, and not knowing
the Irish songs and dances. If only Uncle Brian were
here, he'd see to it."

He had taught the older Belford children to sing and dance at an early age. Katie Rose had learned "Cockles and Mussels" as soon as she could talk.

Jill, with her snub nose and boyish short hair, said, "I don't like showing off. I'd rather sit and eat."

"See that the three of you remember your manners," Ben said.

But he couldn't sound as stern as usual when his bony knees showed between his ribbed socks and short green kilt. Over his white ruffled shirt, he wore the black velvet jacket that had been handed down to him by Grandda O'Byrne; it was cut on the same lines as the fitted white waiter jackets Katie Rose laundered for him to wear at the Ragged Robin.

An appreciative shriek from Stacy announced Miguel's arrival. "I'm *Micky* tonight, Petunia," he announced, "the same as I was called when I lived on the auld sod."

"Micky, it is," she laughed, looking at his reddened nose, green-checked shirt, bow tie, and the unlighted clay pipe that drooped in the corner of his mouth.

For this occasion, he was driving his grandfather's Dodge. He set out with Katie Rose and the three littles. Ben took Mother and Stacy, and stopped en route for Jeanie, who had hurriedly put together an imitation Irish piper costume.

A gala evening! The seven Belfords and their two

guests were met at the door by Guido himself, a stout and bouncy little man with black eyes made for rolling. He ushered the young contingent to a large table while Mother made for the piano. With flourishing bows, he presented green carnation corsages to Katie Rose, Jeanie, Stacy, *and* Jill.

Jill stood ramrod stiff and held it in her hand. Katie Rose pinned it on her shoulder. "Wear it," she scolded in a whisper, "or he'll feel hurt."

"I hate that wilted flowery smell right under my nose," Jill muttered back.

Brian asked, "What about Mom? Has she got flowers to pin on?"

Guido's eyes rolled. "Look on top of the piano. So many people love your mother. Three corsages have come for her. How she can wear them all, I don't know."

A gala and Gaelic evening! Green satin vests on the waiters. Green tablecloths and green candles on the table. "Even the lasagne looks greener tonight," one of the littles commented to the waiter who served them.

"We chop two bales of alfalfa in it for St. Patrick's," he told them. "Other nights we only use one."

"Hah!" said the twins, who knew that one of Guido's relatives devoted his truck farm to raising spinach for the famed lasagne at the Gay Nineties.

In between their dinner and dessert, Ben, Katie Rose, and Stacy danced a jig to their mother's playing "The Irish Washerwoman." They sang "Cockles and Mussels, Alive, Alive-o" with many encores. Requests came thick and fast. Poor Kevin Barry was "hung high upon a gallows tree" in ten stanzas of song.

There was only one thing Katie Rose wished with all her heart: that Mrs. Dujardin was here at Giddy's to see the rollicking response, to realize how Katie Rose Belford could have an audience eating out of her hand, as Guido said.

The musicians took a break, and the young entertainers relaxed at their table. Jeanie, next to Ben, was taking everything in with her bright chipmunk eyes. "Ben, I've never had such a lark," she said, and squeezed his arm. Miguel, who had lived all over the world with his writer father, was speaking Italian to Guido's old mother. She turned to Katie Rose to say, "This is a smart fella you got."

Stacy waved and called out gaily to a near-by diner, "Hello, Mr. Rotharmel that rhymes with carmel."

He came over to their table and pulled up a chair. He asked if the bathroom was finished yet. No, the grand opening was being delayed, they told him. He talked to Ben about his plans for medical school.

He had no sooner rejoined his companions than

Brian asked in a worried manner, "Do you think he's in love with Mother?"

Miguel answered, "Maybe. But don't worry. She still loves her kids the best, though I wouldn't know why."

Stacy leaned over and asked, "Katie Rose, what are you going to get with the money Guido will press in our greedy little paws just as we leave?"

Katie Rose laughed, brimful of happiness. Applause was still ringing in her ears. Her cheeks were bright rose. The world seemed even rosier. She didn't hate Stacy. She didn't hope Bruce would keep on failing in lit. She said, "Oh, I don't know—exactly."

But she did. She'd use the money for a costume or costumes when she took a part in the school play. She asked, "Miguel—I mean Micky—isn't there some quotation about being happy making you good?"

"Yep. 'Oh, make us happy and you make us good.' Browning—not Elizabeth, but Papa—I think."

"I do have a smart fella," she told him. And so easy to be with. Maybe it wouldn't be too hard to push a handsome basketball player out the back door of her heart and slam the door hard.

The next day in drama while the class discussed the purpose of monologue, Katie Rose anxiously waited for the bell—the last of the school day—to ring. She wouldn't ask about the play, because yesterday Mrs. Dujardin had said, "Please, please, don't anyone ask me again if we've decided what play we're putting on. The answer is, Not yet. All I can say is that you'll know as soon as we do."

But as long as Mrs. Dujardin had neither seen nor heard Katie Rose last night, she would surely like to hear about it, wouldn't she? So she pushed her way up to the desk in the front of the room, and said, "Mrs. Dujardin, my brother Ben and my sister and I danced and sang a lot of Irish songs out at Guido's Gay Nineties last night."

"You did? That sounds like fun."

"It was. And talk about audience participation. They all sang with us. We couldn't keep up with all the requests."

She waited, every taut nerve aching to hear, "We'll need talent like yours in the play, Katie Rose." But the drama teacher only sat, absently and wearily tapping the desk with her fingers.

Katie Rose had to go on, "Some of the old-time songs Ben and Stacy didn't know—the words I mean. But once I hear a song, I never forget it. There's that one—it has a sort of haunting lilt—'You Hold My Heart in Your Two Little Hands,' and I sang it alone, and one man out there said he'd give a hundred dollars to have a recording of it—"

Why did someone always have to interrupt? This time it was the librarian who came hurrying into the room with a stack of paperback plays. "I sent downtown for these, Mrs. Dujardin. Looks as if you're in for a lot more reading—and you look pretty bushed."

Mrs. Dujardin walked toward her. "I'll take them home with me. About this time of day I *do* feel bushed. Honestly, I never had such a time getting over a bug."

Mother's elation was the contagious kind. She met Katie Rose at the door that afternoon with a roll of wallpaper in her hand. She evidently had just returned from a shopping tour, for she still had on her coat and gloves.

"Just wait, lovey, just wait till you see! Here, hold this end for me—" She backed away until she had unrolled about five feet of the wallpaper for Katie Rose's inspection. "Did you ever see anything so elegant and arty and Parisian?"

It was no ordinary patterned wall covering. On the background of heavy white paper it was as though an artist had sketched with a blackish-brown pencil two repeating pictures. One was of a shepherd surrounded by a few frolicsome sheep, and the other of a flute player playing for dancing peasants.

"But is it bathroom paper?" Katie Rose asked.

"Lord love us, no! Do you know where you'll see paper just like it? In the foyer of the French Embassy. My friend down at the paint and wallpaper company told me—and he just had this part of a roll left." She laughed in guilty delight. "Even so, I'm scared to tell Ben what I paid for it. Just feel the quality of it. Us, and the French Embassy!"

She carried her paper into the unfinished and desolate space under the stairs, and held it up to the wall with the broken plaster and bare laths showing through. "Um-mm, simply gorgeous! I'll do the papering and painting myself. We won't have this bath of ours looking like just everybody else's bathroom. Because—well, there was something so magical about Grandda getting the fixtures, and Leo finding time—"

Blessed Mom with her driving enthusiasm. Katie Rose beamed at her. "Yes, magical and delightsome, as Stacy says." And again the world seemed delightsome to her.

At that moment Cully set up such a whimpering to get out that Katie Rose stepped to the side door and opened it for him. As she did, she caught a glimpse of a car with a familiar cream-colored body and black top stopping at the corner on the street behind them.

Mother was still talking out her plans from the bathroom, but Katie Rose heard only a car door slam, and saw Cully streak over their fence and make for the corner.

Sure enough, in just the few minutes it would take a girl to walk less than a block, Stacy, with Cully cavorting about her, was turning in their picket gate. So *clandestine*—Bruce's letting her out like that, instead of bringing her home. Rancor flooded through Katie Rose.

Inside, Stacy leaned against the door, flushed and out of breath and glowing. Katie Rose said, "I thought a gentleman was supposed to bring his date to her door, instead of dumping her off on a corner."

Stacy's cheeks flamed even redder. She couldn't answer, for Mother pushed up to show Stacy her wallpaper find.

Katie Rose's up-and-down week. On Sunday morning she stood in the choir beside Stacy. Grudges fairly slid away when a lift of the eyes showed the candles and flowers on the altar and the gentle bowed head of the Virgin. Katie Rose's contralto blended with Stacy's soprano as they sang "Dona nobis pacem" (Give Us Thy Peace). Peace, like soft gray wings, closed over Katie Rose.

That afternoon Stacy answered the phone's ringing. Katie Rose heard only her brief, "Sure I could." She hung up the phone and said, "I'm going to Downey's Drug for more notepaper." That wasn't unusual, for she had covered pages with her "I brought dishonor to St. Jude's. *Mea culpa*—" and still had more to go. Nor was it unusual for Stacy to be gone an hour and a half.

Jeanie and the John-Toms came over that evening. Miguel drifted in. Neither Mother nor Ben worked on Sunday night. Everyone admired the French toile wallpaper. They listened to some new records the John-Toms brought, and Mother showed them how to dance the polka. They all crowded into the dinette for tea and ham sandwiches.

Katie Rose said to Jeanie when she was leaving, "I'm glad this week is over. It's been the *worst* I ever put in," and Jeanie said consolingly, "Next week will be better."

But the next week was not better. It was even worse.

On Monday morning when Miguel stood talking to Katie Rose and Jeanie at their locker, Deetsy came down the hall to hers. She didn't wait to get within speaking distance, but called out, "Hey, Katie Rose, what goes with you and Bruce? I saw him at Downey's Drug yesterday with a luscious little redhead, and they were so buddy-buddy Bruce didn't even see me. I think that's plain crummy when you're helping him pass in lit so he can get back on the team..

The slamming of locker doors ceased, as many girls and a few boys turned to listen for Katie Rose's answer. She could only clutch her weight of books and think, So that's why it took Stacy so long to get her notepaper yesterday.

But Miguel answered in a hearty voice, "That's Katie Rose's sister, didn't you know? Stacy. Haven't you heard about our mutual benefit society? Katie Rose helps Bruce with lit, Stacy helps me with history, Bruce helps Stacy better her basketball game, and I'm teaching Katie Rose to drive."

"That's what I heard," Deetsy said. "And everybody wonders why Bruce doesn't teach her to drive as long as she's helping—"

Jeanie caught that one. "Hah! You tell everybody who wonders that Bruce's mother has a vested interest in the convertible he's driving. And if they knew Mama Seerie, they'd know she isn't the type to let a Learner touch the wheel."

Good work, Miguel. Good work, Jeanie. But it's not good enough for Deetsy. It won't take her long to figure out that Bruce isn't helping Stacy better her basket shooting in Downey's Drug.

Katie Rose had to say something. She could feel everyone waiting. She shrugged and said, "I decided it was a lost cause. Bruce will go through life thinking Shakespeare wrote *Huckleberry Finn*."

No, and it wouldn't take Deetsy, or any interested party, long to realize that Bruce wasn't treating Katie Rose as though they were fellow members in a mutual benefit society. He avoided her assiduously. If they passed in the hall or on the stairs, Bruce, after a first uneasy—even startled—glance, was always very busy looking down at his books, or talking to whoever happened to be by his side.

"You'd think I was Typhoid Mary," Katie Rose told Jeanie with a hollow laugh.

On Wednesday, Mr. Jacoby detained Katie Rose after class. "Well, Kathleen, I want to congratulate you," he said.

"Congratulate me?"

"On your helping Bruce Seerie." His smile was both pleased and conspiratorial. "I must say I never expected a miracle—but what is that saying, 'Never underestimate the power of a woman'? Not that he's an A student—far from it. But it's as though a layer of insulation was ripped off him. On his oral on poetry, he amazed me by coming up with a bit of Whitman. I guess he decided that a man who wrote 'Henceforth, I whimper no more' was someone worth knowing."

"He heard Grandfather and me talking about him," she murmured.

"And I fully expected his autobiography to be duller than—"

"Has he turned it in *already?*"

"Yes, on Monday. You remember I asked for a sort of summing up of what you had learned from life. Bruce admitted that when he'd been put off the team, he had felt resentful toward all of us. But that he had met someone who had made him see the light. He quoted mea culpa—*mea culpa*—"

"Oh-h!" breathed Katie Rose as though a fist had landed in her middle.

Mr. Jacoby misread her exclamation. "I was surprised, too, Kathleen, to have him come up with such an apt Latin phrase."

The final bell rang. Mr. Jacoby, being in an expansive mood, reached for a room-to-room slip to take care of her tardiness to her next class, and went on, "I liked that attitude in Bruce. Because a person's ability to say 'It was my fault' is the first sign of becoming an adult. If he can't say it, he's like the kid who kicks the table leg when he barks his shin on it. And that's what Bruce was, when he nursed a grudge against me for giving him a failing mark, when he nursed the idea that poetry and literature were in the same class as crocheting." He shook his head wonderingly. "You might call it 'The Awakening of Bruce Seerie.' And you, Kathleen, deserve a star in your crown."

She could only stand there with a wooden smile on her lips. She couldn't say, "Don't give me credit for the Awakening of Bruce Seerie. My sister Stacy did that. I didn't have what it takes."

And this was a worse blow than seeing Bruce lifting Stacy off the cement runway by the Purdums' garage, worse than his providing her with ointment for her charley horse—worse even than their being so buddy-buddy at Downey's Drug that Bruce hadn't seen Deetsy. This was a blow to the very roots of her being—Stacy's stirring and inspiring him when *she* couldn't.

She felt an ache in her throat, and the sting of tears behind her eyes. Mr. Jacoby's voice seemed to come from a great distance, "How about your autobiography, Kathleen? The first of April—that's a week from today—is the deadline."

She could only nod and go fumbling out the door with her detained slip. She had to push through the door marked "Girls" and lean against the wall and say aloud to the now empty room, "I couldn't care less." And then she made her way through the quiet hall to the room where Mr. Hill was teaching the *Hallelujah* chorus that would be sung in assembly the Friday before Easter.

After school, Miguel again told her he had his grandfather's car and was going on errands. "So come with me, Petunia. You're pretty good at driving straight ahead. But you need to learn to back, so you can turn or park. That's important."

It didn't seem important now. "Not this afternoon, Miguel. I've—I've got a headache."

"Tomorrow then. And no excuses."

The next day Jeanie walked with them to Miguel's

car. She asked, "Miguel, can't we stop at Katie Rose's house first before the driving lesson? I want to see how near finished the new bath is."

"It's almost," Katie Rose said dully. (Neither did a downstairs bath and shower seem all-important these days.) "Grandda sent in his best carpenter, and Leo brought in a helper to lay the cement floor in the shower. And Mom's been working right along with them." She was silent until she pulled up at the side of her house. "For goodness sake, there's Grandfather Belford's car. I forgot he was coming for tea today."

The shiny Belford car sat in front of the house. Emil, who was general handy man at the Belford mansion as well as chauffeur, waited behind the wheel. (It always troubled Mother to have him sitting there, instead of coming in for tea.)

Grandfather had brought a gift for the new bath. Mother and Ben proudly displayed to Katie Rose, Jeanie, and Miguel an oval mirror, set in a framework of antique gold leaves. "It came from France," Mother said, "and it's an antique."

Grandfather's eyes twinkled. "Not in France, because it's only a hundred years old."

Tea was always more formal when Grandfather came. The big earthenware teapot, the plates of Irish bread—served with Bannon butter that did *not* come in cubes—were brought into the living room. The littles, always a bit awed by the scholarly old gentleman, were on their best behavior.

Mother was pouring tea for the new arrivals when Stacy came hurrying in. She wore that look of radiant excitement Katie Rose had come to think of as her Bruce-look. It rankled.

It rankled, too, when Grandfather, taking his leave, turned at the doorway to say, "Ah, Kathleen, I forgot to inquire as to how your Bruce is getting on with his make-up work in lit."

Her Bruce, indeed! She answered with airy nonchalance, "Mr. Jacoby is practically stunned at how well he's doing. He calls it the Awakening of Bruce Seerie, but I can't claim any credit. He doesn't even look my way any more."

As the door closed behind him, Stacy was saying nervously, "This tea is lukewarm. Should I warm it up, Mom?"

"Never warm up tea," she said. "Always make fresh. Come here, Miguel, and Jeanie, till I show you how the new mirror will look with my elegant French wallpaper."

Leo had set his cup of tea on a convenient sawhorse while he went on working in the bathroom. He backed out so that Mother could display her unrolled wallpaper against the now patched and smooth wall, and Miguel could hold the antique mirror against it.

Jeanie asked, "How much longer will it take?" and Leo answered emphatically, "It's going to be ready the first of April, if I have to bust a G-string."

"Who's going to take the very first shower?" Jeanie wanted to know.

"Matt and Brian and me have been wondering that too," Jill said.

"I," Mother corrected. She added soberly, "That's the momentous question. How are we to decide which one should have the honor of turning on the shower faucets and standing under them for the first time?"

"You, Mom, you should be first," little Brian said.

"Oh no. The last thing I want the first thing in the morning is a shower." Mother gave an exaggerated shudder. "I have to wait and connect with the day."

Stacy called, "I've made fresh tea, everybody."

They all gravitated to the dinette table. Ben said, "How about drawing straws for the Order of the Bath?"

Mother shook her head. "No, it's too great an occasion for drawing straws. What would you think of our taking a secret ballot the night before the first of April? I'll vote, too, so there'll be an uneven number. Only remember, and don't any of you vote for me to christen the bath."

"Sounds like christening a ship by breaking a bottle of champagne on the prow," Miguel said.

"Only we'll break open a box of bath powder," Stacy said.

They sat on at the table, relaxed. Miguel asked Stacy, "Have you finished all your *mea culpas* yet?"

"Almost. I wrote three ball-points dry."

"She's got eleven pages to do still," Jill said importantly. "And you need more notepaper, Stacy."

Katie Rose couldn't let the chance go by to jab Stacy. "It takes her an hour and a half to buy notepaper at Downey's."

She wanted Stacy to look startled and guilty, and she did. Miguel turned reproachful, angry eyes on Katie Rose. Stacy began talking very fast, "A week from Saturday is our wind-up game of the season. And Sister Cabrina says we can celebrate afterwards. She wants us to invite family and friends—our near and dear ones, she calls them. We'll have cake and punch, and dance in the gym. So I'm cordially inviting you all to come and make merry."

Brian pushed up between Jeanie and Ben, and said with his gentle smile, "I want to show you what we found when we cleaned out the closet where the new bathroom is. See, Jeanie, it's a magic slate. Do you know how it works, Ben? You write something with this pencil—only it really isn't a pencil—and then you lift up this white waxy paper and it's gone."

"Let me try it," Ben said.

Katie Rose, sitting next to him, saw the words he wrote for Jeanie's eyes, "Will you go to the near-and-dear party at St. Jude's with me?" Katie Rose saw Jeanie write back, "With the greatest of pleasure." Ben lifted the top sheet of opaque white paper and the words disappeared.

Miguel reached for it next and wrote, "Petunia, how about us going to Stacy's game and dance afterwards?" and handed it to her. She thought only of Bruce's being there, of his cheering each time Stacy made a basket. She wrote in large words, "No, thank you. I can't think of any place I'd rather *not* go," and passed it back to him. He lifted the page to clear it and wrote another message for her. It was, "I could bash your teeth in."

It wasn't only the words but his scorching eyes under their sandy lashes that jolted her. This, from Miguel who always said, "I guess it's in the stars, Petunia, that whenever either of us needs help the other will come running." Their first meeting had been when he appeared at the Belford door, tattered and hungry, after driving up from Mexico and finding his grandparents gone on a trip. "I was hungry and you gave me food," he said. And on last Hallowe'en night when Katie Rose had taken the little McHarg girls out for Trick or Treat, and some hoodlum boys were giving them a frightening time, it was Miguel who had miraculously appeared and sent the offenders on their way.

She had never thought it was in the stars for Miguel to want to bash her teeth in. She obliterated his message on the magic slate and handed it back to Brian.

Jeanie stood up, and Ben said he would drive her home. She said from the doorway, "You'll do better on your backing and turning without me, Katie Rose."

Stacy and the littles went their way. Mother was busy with Leo. Only Katie Rose and Miguel were left at the dinette table. Under cover of the hammering in the bathroom, Miguel demanded, "Are you proud of all those poison darts you aimed at Stacy?"

"What do you think I should do? Pin a medal on her?"

"Never mind the curled lip. It doesn't do a thing for you. Just tell me this: Why are you giving her the works because she and Bruce like each other?"

Put thus bluntly, it was hard to answer without admitting, "Because he's always been special to me. Because I've always wanted to be his girl."

She didn't meet his accusing eyes, but turned her cup round and round in the saucer. "They're so sneaky about it. He meets her at school and instead of bringing her home, he lets her off on the corner back of us."

"You know why. Because of the outraged act you're putting on. I think it's too darn' bad he couldn't come home with her and have tea with all of us."

"Go ahead and side with Stacy."

"I'm not siding with anybody. Bruce is a good joe. He tells you about Jacoby failing him, and you try to help him. That doesn't mean you *own* him, does it? So you've decided to stay home and sulk next Saturday, hoping you'll spoil the game and party for Stacy."

That was too much. Spoil the afternoon for Stacy! What hadn't Stacy spoiled for her? Her voice rose. "You're overlooking—" The noisy hammering came to a halt. She pulled her voice down and started over, and this time her lips were definitely curled, "You're overlooking who the invitation is for. 'The near and dear ones'—remember? Well, there's nothing near and dear between Stacy and—"

There it was again—the ache in her throat and the hot push of tears. She got up quickly and fled out of the dinette. And there it was again—no place where a girl could flee to and shed tears in private. She went up the stairs, but not to *their* room where Stacy was engaged on those endless *mea culpas*. Not to Ben's room, for he would be home any minute. She sought brief haven in the littles' room with its odorous tenants of white mice in a homemade cage and turtles in a bowl of murky water.

There was no driving lesson that afternoon.

At five o'clock on Friday, Katie Rose waited in the hall at home to be picked up by Mr. Barton who would take her to spend the evening with his wife's elderly mother.

The phone rang, and Katie Rose picked it up to hear Deetsy's shrill, gushy voice, "I've got news for you, hon. Mrs. Du told Howie and Howie told me what play they're putting on."

"Which one, Deetsy?"

"*Come to My Arms, Marybelle.*"

"*Come to My Arms*— Oh goody. I've seen it and it's—"

"Mrs. Du told Howie and Howie told me that one reason they took it was because most of the costumes could be made in sewing. You know it opens with a picnic and they do square dances, and those dresses are just full skirts and bodices." Deetsy was enjoying her role of being-in-the-know. "And besides, the music isn't too hard for the school except for one—"

"Here's Mr. Barton stopping for me." But Katie Rose had to take time to ask, "Deetsy, did Howie say anything to you about my tryout?"

"Oh yes, he said you were a wow. He said you and that stuck-up little Zoe were the best of all the girls. Everybody knows that."

On those heartening words, Katie Rose opened the door for Mr. Barton.

She always enjoyed her evenings with Mrs. Barton's mother who was so crippled up with arthritis she had to get about in a wheelchair. She always thought of it as her Eva-sitting job. For the old lady had said to her on her first evening there, "Do you know, Katie Rose, the one thing old people miss? It's hearing their first name. I'm Mother and Grandma and Mrs. Webster, but all the ones who called me Eva are either dead or far from here." She ended wistfully, "Eva. Nobody ever calls me that, and sometimes I feel as though I've lost part of my identity."

"I'll call you Eva," Katie Rose promised.

Nor was Eva a docile and resigned old woman in a wheelchair. She was vain and frivolous, and had a salty wit. This evening, her plain, sensible daughter showed Katie Rose the patties of chopped round steak to be broiled and the carrots to be mashed for their supper. As she set out the applesauce and murmured, "At Mother's age, she needs food that's easy to digest," the old lady gave Katie Rose a roguish wink.

They both watched out the window as the middle-aged Bartons got in the car and drove off for their buffet supper and evening of bridge. Then Eva asked with bright mischievous eyes, "What shall we order tonight, Katie Rose?" She had also exploded to her, "Millie, and her blah-blah digestible food!" She always had Katie Rose phone for Mexican or Chinese dinners to be delivered, or sometimes for barbecued ribs from the Ragged Robin.

This evening they decided on Chinese food. "Tell them a double order of shrimp, with lots of hot sauce," Eva prompted.

That was the first part of their evening's routine. Next, Katie Rose wheeled her into the bathroom and shampooed her hair. From the top dresser drawer she took the bottle of tint which turned Eva's almost-white hair to a chocolate brown. Katie Rose then put it up on rollers. Eva's daughter didn't approve of this procedure, but Mr. Barton said, "Oh now, Millie, if the old lady wants it that way—" And Eva liked to tell Katie Rose that one of her beaux had once told her her hair was the same color as his bay roping horse.

Usually it was Eva who did the talking—about the box suppers, Maypole dances, Fourth of July picnics she had gone to in her young days and where, according to her telling, she had been the undisputed belle. But this evening, Katie Rose was so brimful of *Come to My Arms, Marybelle*, she had to tell about it.

"It's a lovely, lovely play, Eva. Last summer our

whole family saw it at the theater at Acacia Gardens. It was on Friday when Mom and Ben were off work—"

"What's it about?"

"It's about a man, Danny, that comes back to a garment house where he was just a stock boy before he left to go West and make his fortune. And he did. He came back in ten or twelve years as a big cattle-man—"

"Huh! In real life, it'd take forty. My husband raised cattle, and the first ten years we nearly starved."

"He came back to marry Marybelle, who was a beautiful model whom he loved. But he couldn't find her because—"

"She'd had time to marry and have five or six kids."

"Oh no—she didn't marry. She was right there at the garment factory. But she'd been in a car accident or something, and she limped, so now she just did alterations. And here was this Danny seeking his beautiful Marybelle who could dance like a leaf in the wind, and so she—looking so drab and beat—wouldn't come forward and say, 'Here I am.' I've been counting in my mind and besides Marybelle, there're four supporting parts for girls. Every one of them makes a play for Danny because he's rich and they—"

"Bobby pins for my bangs," Eva reminded her.

Katie Rose went on as she rimmed Eva's forehead with tight little snails of curls, "There's a mercenary little model who wants him because he has money in the bank. She does a song and, like Hamlet, she appeals to the audience, 'What do you think? Wouldn't I be sen-sa-tion-al in mink?' "

"Ermine was all the rage when I was young," Eva reminisced.

"Then there is the model who had to starve herself to keep her weight down. Her name is Myrtle. She asks Danny if he has cows that give whipped cream. It's a cute, cute part where she dances and sings a crazy song about Myrtle and her girdle. She waves it and sings, 'Hurray! Hurray! I'll throw my girdle away.' "

"Right here, honey—this roller pulls too tight. What are the other parts?"

"They aren't so good. One is a cowgirl who shows up at the picnic. Sort of an Annie-Get-Your-Gun type with spurs and a loud voice. She tries to tell Danny what a help she'd be to him on his cattle ranch. Then there's the manager's wife—the jealous old harpy—always pulling her husband away from the pretty models."

"Maybe you'll get the lead. What is it now—Annabelle?"

"Marybelle." That was the part her mind lingered

on. Marybelle, the careworn "alterations" to whom the models tossed dresses with, "Hurry, and let this out a little," or "Fix the zipper for me."

She mused aloud, "The final scene is so beautiful—everybody in the audience cries. Poor little 'alterations'—only she's really Marybelle—comes out of her cubbyhole after the fashion show is over and everyone is gone. She takes off her eyeshade and puts on a beautiful dress, and dances there all alone—the same dance she danced with Danny before he left. And he comes in—"

"And recognizes his lost love," Eva chortled.

"Yes. He holds out his arms to dance with her but she backs off from him and says, 'I limp when I dance. I limp when I walk,' and he says, 'I can match my step to yours,' and they dance together."

The delivery of their Chinese supper interrupted her. She wheeled Eva to the table. "I'm not counting on the lead. I'm sure Zoe will get that."

"When will they give out the parts?"

"Most any day. Our drama teacher has said all along the parts would be given out before the first of April."

Another part of Katie Rose's routine with Eva was the destroying of all evidence of their sent-in meal. She carried the cartons to the ashpit and burned them.

She washed the dishes and wiped up every spatter of soy sauce from the table and floor.

Eva said, "You've got a dog, haven't you? He ought to like that chewed-up meat Milly left for us."

"I'll say. He'll think it's Christmas. He eats everything except old inner tubes."

It was now Eva's turn to tell of her young and sought-after days. Katie Rose listened and said, "Just think!" or "Goodness, I'll bet you looked pretty," in the right places, but her mind was still on *Come to My Arms, Marybelle.*

Monday, the twenty-ninth of March. The parts for the play were not yet posted.

Tuesday, the thirtieth of March. At lunchtime Deetsy said, "Mrs. Du told Howie and Howie told me that she and Pete Hill and the sewing teacher—and I don't know who else—are going into a final hassle tonight—"

"Tomorrow's the last day of March," Katie Rose said shakily, "and Mrs. Dujardin has said all along—"

"That's why the hassle. So the cast can be posted for the seventh hour Drama Club meeting in the greenroom tomorrow."

The next day when Katie Rose left Mr. Jacoby's lit class her heart was pounding like a trip hammer in her throat. Other pupils were turning in the story of their lives, but not she. How could a girl write about her life when she was suspended between a high cloud and the earth? Her story would have to wait till tomorrow for its final summing up. She had already written:

"My heart's desire is to be an actress. And now I feel that my feet are set on the first rung of the ladder because in our musical comedy I am to play—"

No, she must *not* imagine herself in the part of Marybelle. Zoe would be given that. But she had every right to imagine herself in one of the other roles.

Clasping her weight of books tightly, she walked down the hall and through the side door to the auditorium and into the milling crowd in the greenroom. A knot of students was gathered around the call board and the thumb-tacked list on it.

Two boys made way for her so that she was within reading distance, and her eyes focused on the names. Sure enough, there was Zoe's name opposite the part of Marybelle. She had known that all along, she told herself. That was no disappointment. But she said a wistful farewell to herself and her dancing alone in the dark old factory—alone until Danny came in.

The next part was that of the model who in the play would ask Danny, "If you can't find Marybelle, wouldn't I do?" She was the one who asked the audience if it didn't think she'd look sen-sa-tion-al in mink. A girl in the drama class named Sharon had been chosen as the mercenary model.

But Myrtle who "was sick of being strangled by a girdle," who wanted her fill of whipped cream with never a worry about a seam— Ah, next to the lead, Katie Rose would rather have the part of Myrtle. But Linda Little was written opposite it. Of all things! Linda was in girls' choir with Katie Rose; her voice wasn't anything to brag about. Katie Rose fought against a sense of outrage that Linda, not Katie Rose, was to play Myrtle.

The next female character was Mrs. Diekvoss. Mrs. Diekvoss? Oh yes, the nagging, sharp-tongued wife of the dress factory owner. Not a very good part. Josephine somebody had been given it.

The only role left was that of the cowgirl. It wasn't a pretty or a dressy part, but a rowdy, loud-voiced one. Maybe Mrs. Dujardin had decided on Katie Rose for it because it was a hard part to get over. A girl's bouffant hair-do pushed between her and the printed list. And in that instant, she had a flashing vision of how she could put herself over in the part. She would borrow a ten-gallon hat and a fringed buckskin jacket from some of their rodeo friends in Bannon. Yes, and spurs. Jangling spurs would add a lot to her dance.

The bouffant hair-do bobbed aside, and Katie

Rose's eyes rested on the name opposite the Ride-'em-high part. She couldn't believe it. She couldn't believe that the last decent part had been given to a girl named Darlene McClough. She couldn't believe that the name Katie Rose Belford was not on the list of parts for *Come to My Arms, Marybelle.*

Deetsy pushed up to her. "Oh, here you are, Katie Rose. Did you see?—you're down here with the eight girls who're to dance in the square dance at the picnic. There'll be two sets. I'm there too," she added with a squeal of delight. "I'm just tickled to death. Like I say, I can't sing and I can't act, but I can dance. I'll bet sweet old Howie helped to get me on. But he said he couldn't understand why Mrs. Du— He's said all along you were tops in the tryouts."

She, Katie Rose, to fill up the stage and add color and background! She had tumbled from her high cloud onto hard ground, and her breath was knocked out of her.

Her knees were suddenly mush. She had to turn away from the call board and Deetsy and fumble her way to a seat. A girl was slumped in a chair near her, and she said, "Oh hi, Katie Rose." It was Zoe, her heavy blond braid raveled out at the end. Zoe had the lead. Zoe had the world by the tail. She could afford to relax in bliss while everyone else milled about.

I'm not actress enough, a stunned Katie Rose

thought, to smile and congratulate her. She could only say on a labored breath, "I guess you saw—Mrs. Du put me down for one of the square dancers."

Zoe turned her druid's eyes on her. "A dancing part is pure fun, Katie Rose. I mean you don't have a part to learn or worry about making a mistake. Actresses always say you learn more about how a play is put on when you have a background part. One summer I was one of the dancers in *Carousel*. You know there's a picnic in it too."

Never mind trying to soften the blow, Zoe.

"I wore one of those quadrille dance dresses in it, Katie Rose. I've got an aunt who sews, and she went all out on it. It's a violet print and there're miles in the skirt, and the round neck has sort of puckery ruffles so that it looks like a purple and white lei. And every time I see you, I think how that purplish dress would be so right with your purplish eyes—"

She paused for an answer. None came, and Zoe blurted out, "I'd like you to wear my violet dress to dance in."

Zoe felt sorry for her! Anger pushed through Katie Rose's jolted numbness—not hot anger, but anger like cracked ice in her middle. She said with cold courtesy, "Thanks, Zoe, but I'm not going to be a background dancer." She even managed an indifferent laugh.

"They won't have any trouble replacing me. Square dancers are a dime a dozen."

She hurled herself out of the seat and started for the door. Mrs. Dujardin and the sewing teacher were holding sketches of costumes in their hands and discussing them. As Katie Rose pushed past, the drama teacher said, "Oh, Katie Rose! Just a minute, I want to talk to you."

She took her arm and drew her aside. "You're disappointed, aren't you?"

Katie Rose's face remained stony, though she longed to hurl out, "What did you think I'd be? You were the one who urged me to take drama because you said I had unusual talent. I gave up swimming to take it, and I've read every play you've even mentioned. I've saved the ten dollars I got St. Patrick's night for costumes even though I have to go on wearing these tennis shoes with William J. Purdum still showing through. You said my tryout was good, very good, and now—now—"

Mrs. Dujardin was asking, "Did you talk to your grandfather about the system they used in giving out parts to the Abbey players?"

"I haven't seen my grandfather lately."

"Then let me tell you the point he emphasized when—"

"Never mind. Let me tell you that you can give my dancing part to someone else, Mrs. Dujardin."

The teacher started to say, "I don't think you mean that," but Katie Rose bolted out of the door. She couldn't bear to be in the room. She couldn't face anyone else saying, as Deetsy had, "Everybody was sure you'd get one of the good parts."

Jeanie was waiting at the locker. She looked at the tragic misery in her friend's face and said, "I heard about it, Katie Rose. Deetsy told me."

"Old Walkie-talkie! I don't suppose there's anyone in the whole school she hasn't told."

"Come on, Katie Rose, and walk home with me. This is Mom's afternoon at Mt. Carmel nursery, and we'll make us some cocoa. It's cold and dreary out." Her words didn't say it but her eyes did, "I ache with you, Katie Rose." She added, "Let's get out of here before the final bell rings and the mob takes over."

Katie Rose flung open the locker. Under the mirror on the inside of the door, the two girls had fastened a plastic pocket to hold combs, lipsticks, pencils. Katie Rose was hurriedly divesting it of her belongings.

"What in the world are you taking all that stuff for?" Jeanie asked.

Katie Rose opened her tight lips. "Because I never intend to put foot in this school again. I'll leave all my books and this other stuff at your house."

"Oh now, Katie Rose, don't be a goose girl."

Katie Rose went right on piling on top of her books an extra pair of mittens, her swimsuit, and the roll of rose denim left over from the skirt she had just finished in sewing. Jeanie said, "Here, let me carry some of your load. Better button your coat. Whoever said March would go out like a lion, said a mouthful. Looks like snow again."

Katie Rose didn't button her coat, but walked uncaring through the wide glass doors and into the chilling wind. Jeanie waited until they had passed a few knots of students and when they were out of earshot, she said, "I can't imagine Mrs. Du not giving you a better part. She always seemed to think you were such a find. She asked you to join her class because—"

"I don't have to imagine anything," Katie Rose flung out. "I *know*. She gave it away herself when she admitted she knew my grandda O'Byrne when she was in teachers' college. She was in a play he directed. And sure as sin, she expected a good, juicy part, and he didn't give it to her. And so she's taking it out on me."

"Oh now, Katie Rose, she—"

"Don't oh-now-Katie-Rose me. I can remember plain as day how—how sort of taken back she was when I told her he was my grandfather. Right then she changed. Up to then, she'd been so palsy-walsy—

oh dear me, butter wouldn't melt in her mouth. Hypo-critical old hippopotamus!"

"Did she say anything about why she just gave you a dance part?"

"She was spouting some senseless stuff about the Abbey players, and did I ever ask Grandda how they managed there. None of it made sense. I told her she could take her old swing-on-the-corner part and give it to the first person she met. I've had it."

Jeanie said thoughtfully, "Katie Rose, I know this seems like the end of the world to you now. You think every boy and girl at Adams will know you counted on getting a good part, and didn't—"

"And will make some wisecrack about it," Katie Rose put in.

"But who? The ones in art are up to their ears getting ready for their exhibit. The ones on the paper can't think of anything but getting out the paper before spring vacation. I know it's a terrible blow right now. But no one should decide on something drastic when she's— Well, you know, 'First take counsel of your pillow'—meaning to sleep on it, because then—"

Katie Rose turned on her fiercely, "Will you please just listen to me? Will you please spare me the philosophy?"

Again Jeanie looked at her with understanding. "All right, go ahead. I won't say a word."

"I will not give Dujardin a chance to gloat over me. I will not have Zoe feeling lordly and sympathetic, and offering me a purple dress some old aunt made her—"

"I think it was nice of her. And so will you when you cool off. And you'll look like a doll in it."

"I never intend to lay eyes on her or Dujardin. I'm going home with you, and I'm going to phone Uncle Brian in San Francisco. I'll call him at his TV store, and I'll tell him I've got to come out right away. I'll ask him to wire me the fare. I don't care how I go, by plane, train, or bus. I'll go down to Western Union and wait for the money, and whichever leaves first, I'll be on it. All I want is to get out of this town and be on my way."

"You'll have to go home first. You'll need to change clothes and pack."

"I'll go in what I've got on." But Katie Rose wished she weren't wearing her faded blue slipover and pleated skirt, her Purdum tennis shoes and ribbed socks. She would have worn her purple jumper and ruffled blouse if she had been able to launder it this morning. But Leo, attaching pipes for the new bath, had turned the water off.

"And I will not go home. I told all of them I was sure of a good part in the show. I told the McHargs—and Eva—" Her voice threaded, but inner fury bodied it up. "Do you think I'm going to go home and say, 'Oh, you'll be so proud of me. I'm one of the twenty or so in the background. If you borrow opera glasses and look close, you might be able to tell which one is me.' Do you think I want Stacy saying to Bruce, 'Oh, poor Katie Rose. You mustn't ever drive me to the front door. Her heart is broken enough'?"

She paused for breath and for a remark from Jeanie. None was forthcoming, and she added, "Every time I've talked to Uncle Brian on the phone, he says he's homesick for a sight of me. He calls me his bright angel—" Again her voice lumped.

"You are his bright angel. But, Katie Rose, go home and talk it over with your mother. And then phone him from there."

"Can I use your phone or can't I? It'll be a collect call, so you won't have to worry about—"

"Katie Rose! I'm not worrying about any telephone bill, for heaven's sake."

Katie Rose walked on, her jaw set and eyes narrowed. Oh, to step off a plane, train, or bus in a strange city far, far from Denver. Oh, to have Uncle Brian's strong arms swing her off the ground and to hear his, "Mavourneen! You're a sight for sore eyes."

She said loudly, "He can't wait to take me to his Lady Gregory theater group. He said they needed an *ingenue* type."

Her lacerated ego focused on that. The Lady Gregory group would cast her in a play and be amazed at how she captivated her audience. . . . From ingenue she would move up to stardom and spectacular success. . . . She pictured herself being interviewed by an eager and awed reporter. She heard herself say on a gay, confident laugh, "You've heard of blessings in disguise? You see, when I was sixteen our drama teacher vented her personal spite on me by not giving me a part in the school play. It seemed terribly important to me at the time, and yet—" again the carefree, rippling laugh, "had it not been for that, I would never have come to San Francisco—"

Beside her, Jeanie exclaimed, "For gosh sakes, there's Johnny Malone! See, talking to Beany Buell in front of her house. Looks as if they're waiting for us."

Johnny hurried across the lawn to them. "Katie Rose, you're a lifesaver. We've been calling your house but your mother said you weren't home from school yet. Beany said she'd bet you were walking home with Jeanie. Please, Katie Rose, could you baby-sit our little Melody for Miggs and me tonight?"

She heard the words but they didn't make sense. For she had to transplant herself from an exquisitely furnished apartment in San Francisco to a pavement in Harmony Heights, from a famous star in a hostess gown of orchid velvet to a baby-sitter in a plaid skirt and shabby tennis shoes.

16

Katie Rose could only
stare stupidly at Beany and Johnny while Beany explained that tonight was the night of the oil men's
banquet at which Johnny was to be honored because
of his TV program on the oil industry in Colorado.

Johnny explained further, "I don't know whether
you know, Katie Rose, but Miggs's father, Mr. Carmody, is one of the big wheels in the oil men's associa-
tion. He flew up from Texas for the doings tonight.
At first Miggs didn't plan on going, but Mr. Carmody
wouldn't hear to her staying home."

"Of course not," Jeanie said. "She ought to be there
to see them present you with a bronze plaque."

Johnny grinned. "I'd sooner they presented me
with an oil change for my car."

Everyone laughed at that except Katie Rose. She

walked with the others into Beany's house out of the
raw, chill air. Beany said, "I could go out and stay
with little Melody, only the doctor thinks I should
stay close to home at this stage of the game." They
laughed at that, too, and Katie Rose thought, Nothing
seems funny to me right now.

"So could you help them out, Katie Rose, as long as
I can't?" Beany asked. "Or had you planned something else this evening?"

She had planned to take a plane, train, or bus out of
town. She said, "I'll have to see. I'll have to make a
phone call."

Beany motioned to the telephone on the low divi-
sion between living room and kitchen. "Go ahead and
use it."

But Katie Rose didn't want them to know the nature of her call. Jeanie came to the rescue. "She
planned to phone from our house. Here's my key,
Katie Rose."

She let herself into the empty Kincaid house. She
went to Jeanie's room, sat on the bed, and reached for
the pale blue phone she had always envied Jeanie. She
dialed long distance, and said she wanted to place a
collect call to Brian O'Byrne in San Francisco. She
gave the name and address of the TV store of which
Uncle Brian was manager.

She waited tensely while the Denver operator ob-

tained the number from San Francisco information.
She heard the few rings at the San Francisco store
before a man's voice answered. Disappointment. Brian
O'Byrne was not in the store. When was he expected
back? He might not be back before closing time; he
had gone to a sales conference.

Katie Rose replaced the telephone. Then she might
as well go out to the farm with Johnny and stay with
little Melody while her father was banqueted and honored. She, Katie Rose, would wait until she was alone
with the baby, and then call Uncle Brian at his apartment.

She walked across the lawn to the Buell house next
door, and told Johnny that yes, she could baby-sit for
them. "You can call Mom back and tell her."

"Wouldn't you rather call her?" Beany asked.

Katie Rose shook her head. She didn't want her
mother asking her what part she had been given in the
show.

Johnny phoned. And Mother, being Mother, was all
friendliness and well wishes. She had seen the write-
up in the paper about Mr. Carmody flying up from
Texas in his private plane to present the award to his
son-in-law.

Johnny apologized for its being a school night, but
assured her they wouldn't be out late because Miggs
was still the baby's meal ticket. He handed the phone

to Katie Rose. "She wants to speak to her ever-lovin' daughter."

Oh-oh. Here was the question Katie Rose dreaded. But Mother's mind was too full of the downstairs bath to give thought to who had been given what role in *Come to My Arms, Marybelle*. The hot and cold water were now attached in the shower, although Leo was having trouble getting a rumble out of the hot. And just wait until Katie Rose saw the vanity shelf that encased the corner washbowl under the mirror with its filigree gold frame. "It's like having a shower for the shower. More people have sent presents. The most beautiful cut-glass bottles came from—now what is that fellow's name that only Stacy can remember?"

"You mean Rotharmel?"

Everyone in the Buell house heard Mother's hearty laugh. "Of course, to rhyme with Stacy's carmel. I won't be late tonight—Wednesdays are never so busy at Giddy's. So all of you wait up, and then we'll cast the secret ballots for the lucky one who gets to take the first shower in the morning."

What a queer, detached feeling Katie Rose had as she listened. There would be one Belford vote short tonight. Mother was saying, "I wish Stacy would get home so I can send her down to the Boulevard for a shower cap. I can't imagine what's keeping her."

The listener's lips thinned. She could. Stacy and Bruce would be dawdling over cokes at Downey's Drug. Let them, let them! By this time tomorrow Katie Rose would be far removed from all that.

She said loudly, "Well, good-by, Mom," and thought as she hung up, The next call you hear from me will be from San Francisco.

The hospitable Beany wanted to make them all coffee or tea, but Johnny said that he and Katie Rose had better be on their way.

"Your books, Katie Rose," Beany reminded her. "Did you leave them in Jeanie's house when you phoned?"

"I don't want them." Let the math and French books gather dust. Let the autobiography of Kathleen Rose Belford go forever unfinished—heart's desire, summing up, and all.

Jeanie pushed close to her as they walked to Johnny's car. "Did you get Uncle Brian?"

"He wasn't at the store. I'll call him from the farm. I know his apartment number. And I'm counting on you not to say a word to my folks about anything." She turned away from the troubled concern in Jeanie's eyes.

Beany called from the doorway, "Johnny, get your

hair cut. You can't go to a banquet and receive a bronze trophy with your hair over your eyes like a sheepdog's."

"That woman!" he said as he helped Katie Rose into the car. "She's a Greek chorus of one with her 'Johnny, get your hair cut.'"

They drove off. Katie Rose didn't look back. She didn't want to think that she wouldn't see Jeanie again —maybe not for years.

Johnny glanced at her as he stopped at the first red light. "Everything going all right for you, Katie Rose?"

"Everything will be fine after tonight," she said briefly.

"Your boy friend, Miguel, came out after eggs again yesterday. We were sorry you weren't along to visit with us."

Not my boy friend, she thought dully. Not since last Thursday when he said he could bash my teeth in. . . . Well, what did he expect her to do? Go crawling to him and say, "I'll change my ways. I'll be in ec-stacy over Stacy's and Bruce's big romance"? But the weekend had been strangely lacking without Miguel bobbing in. These few intervening days he had sat at the same noisy lunch table with her and behind her in study hall and, while no outsider could notice a difference, Katie Rose could. He was polite and withdrawn. He hadn't mentioned a driving lesson or how she needed to learn to back and turn a car. . . .

She answered Johnny, "I've been pretty busy."

He talked on, "Miggs gets such a wallop out of selling eggs. It drives her father crazy. But then he's got so much dough, he doesn't know they make anything less than ten-dollar bills."

She couldn't seem to make conversation. Under her hurt and humiliation, plans kept churning. When Uncle Brian flew to California in early January he had taken a plane around midnight; she remembered because they had all gone to the airport to see him off. If Johnny and Miggs came home about ten—

Johnny was saying, "You've heard about drooling grandparents. Grandpa Carmody heads the list. If he can find any excuse to fly up here, he does just to see our Melody. He had a business meeting around noon today, and I'll bet a dollar to a doughnut he took a taxi to the farm, and we'll walk in and find him cooing and clucking over her. I'd better stop here at the junction for gas."

He pulled into the station, and waited until two cars were serviced. He greeted the man who came hurrying up, "Busy as usual, Curt? Thought you were going to get a helper."

Curt shook his head ruefully while the gas gurgled into the tank. "I got one. But I'm not sure whether he's a help or a hindrance. He's supposed to be here at four—four to midnight—but he hasn't showed yet."

Johnny reached for the change Curt gave him. He stood, holding his gloved palm out to them. "Look at that, Katie Rose. Do you see it, Curt?" He was showing them a single snowflake, fragile as a miniature cobweb and with an intricate geometric design, resting lightly beside the quarter and dime. Johnny said wonderingly, "That's a little harbinger that came down in advance to tell us there are a lot more where it came from. Sort of a warning for everyone to hunt up overshoes and see if windshield wipers work."

Curt chuckled. "Somebody was telling me that March would go out like a lion because it came in like a lamb."

Was it only a month ago Katie Rose's math teacher had quoted that? It seemed eons ago. March had come in with such wonderful promise; March was going out with every hope blasted.

As Johnny got into the car, Katie Rose saw among the numerous shops and stores at the junction the striped pole of a barbershop, and she asked, "Are you going to get a haircut?"

"Not if I can help myself. Miggs isn't the kind to make an issue of it."

They drove on. A few leisurely, swirling flakes misted on the windshield by the time they turned off the main road and into the lane that led to the apple-green farmhouse. They stopped and Johnny said, "As long as you were here before, I don't need to tell you that we always use the back door while the front is rusting on its hinges. And here comes our milkmaid."

Here came Miggs, her brown hair dotted with snow-flakes. He took the bucket of milk from her, and she gave Katie Rose her warm, shy smile. "I told Johnny you were the only one I'd be willing to leave the baby with."

He had guessed right when he said their baby's grandfather would be there, cooing over the baby. Little Melody lay on a pink blanket on the couch in the big, cozy kitchen. Mr. Carmody sat beside her, making clucking sounds just to see her kick and flail her arms and legs. He said proudly, "You know I think she knows me. She laughed the minute I bent over her."

But Johnny was not to escape a trip to the barber-shop. Miggs didn't say it, but Mr. Carmody did, "You'd better get your hair cut before the big shindig tonight."

Johnny winked at Katie Rose. "All right, if I have to I have to. I'll drive back to the junction and get one."

"Better tell them to hurry. It's after five now," Mr. Carmody said.

"The banquet isn't until seven," Miggs reminded him in her unruffled way.

She carried the milk into the big pantry off the kitchen. "I left out this panful of milk to skim for cream," she said.

"I know how to skim off cream," Katie Rose said. "You go ahead and dress for your party."

Miggs laughed. "I'm one of these awful females who can shower and dress in fifteen minutes. We'll leave the baby's bassinet behind the base-burner in the dining room. And by the way, if old Charley drops in to listen to TV, don't let him turn it up full blast. He's an old-time bronco buster who used to work for us, but now he's all crippled up from an auto accident. We have him living in what was once a bunkhouse, and he has a few favorite programs he comes over to watch."

Katie Rose was skimming the thick cream off the milk, and the shower was humming in the bathroom, when someone rapped at the kitchen door. Mr. Carmody, still on the couch with the baby, called out, "Come in. Come in."

The door opened and a big man with slouching shoulders stepped into the kitchen, bringing with him the smell of wet, unclean clothes and an unpleasant odor from the cigar in his mouth. He said, "I saw in the paper you was in town, Carmody. I figured you'd be out here."

Mr. Carmody turned his gaze from the baby to the caller. "Hello, Dawson," he said, without getting up and without welcome in his greeting.

Dawson didn't take off his shapeless black hat, but pushed it back on his unkempt head. He repeated, "Yeh, I saw where you was going to be at a banquet tonight and so—"

"What do you want, Dawson?"

"You know what I want. I want you to give me my job back. I'm entitled to it. That's what I come out here for." Strange that a voice could be both belligerent and whining.

Mr. Carmody stood up. He was shorter than his visitor. When Katie Rose had seen him first, she had thought he looked more like an easygoing farmer than an oil tycoon. But seeing him now from the pantry, she realized the hard, relentless core under his easy exterior. He said curtly, "No man is entitled to a job he can't hold down. Dawson, I've fired you three times because you deserved it. I hired you back twice, because I wanted to give you every chance. Haven't you got a job?"

"Job!" the big man spat out. "I'm wiping windshields and shoveling snow at a little dump of a filling station. Call that a job? I'm an oil-rigger, and you know it."

"You *were* an oil-rigger." Katie Rose saw Carmody's shrewd eyes taking in the man's rumpled clothes, his mottled face, the shaky fingers that brandished the odorous stub of cigar before he tossed it into the coal scuttle. "You were an oil-rigger before you started drinking—"

"Drinking!" the man sneered. "I take a little drink now and then same as everybody else."

"—and I've told you dozens of times that oil and booze don't mix. If I gave you a job you'd only pull another blunder that would cost me plenty."

"You always blamed me for everything. Every time some of your machinery went haywire, you blamed me."

Mr. Carmody gave a short laugh. "Well, you never blamed yourself. Why don't you wake up, Dawson? Why don't you put the blame on yourself? Or is it easier to blame *me* for your being down and out?"

"It's your fault that my wife picked up my boys and left me," Dawson accused. "You put her up to it."

"That's right. She came to me for help, and I took one look at her bruises and the welts on your boys. I gave her money and told her to get as far away as she could."

The baby on the blanket took that moment to give a gurgling crow, and her grandfather bent over her with a loving smile. He even took a minute to pull the bootee back on the small foot that had kicked it off.

The caller said—and now his voice was all snarl, "I want the promise of a job from you. You owe it to me. And I'm telling you this, Carmody, you'll be sorry if you don't—"

Mr. Carmody's voice was cutting. "You're stupider than I thought, Dawson, if you think you can threaten me. I don't scare easy. Now get out. I'm even wasting time listening to a man who's been hitting the bottle all day."

The man opened the door, held it open while a blasphemous and poisonous tirade came out of his raspy throat. He wasn't the kind of a man to be kicked around—he'd show Carmody—he'd make him eat dust—

Mr. Carmody wrenched the door out of his hand. In an ominously quiet voice he said, "The draft from the door is hitting the baby. I'll close it after you."

He closed it firmly. From the pantry door, Katie Rose listened to the rattle of the car's starting and driving off. Miggs came out of the bathroom, her hair damp at the edges, bundling a robe about her.

"Who was that, Dad?"

"A fellow named Dawson. I've always said I didn't

know which was the worse to deal with—a knave or a fool. And Dawson is both. It's too far back for you to remember, Miggs, but he used to live on a little acreage near here. When I first went into the oil business in Oklahoma, he followed me down. That's why I've given him every chance. He won't admit he's a drunk. He won't admit it was his fault that his poor wife picked up their kids and left him. He's a destructive man."

Mr. Carmody picked the cigar butt out of the coal scuttle and tossed it out the door. "There's nothing better than the smell of a good cigar, and nothing —so help me!—can turn your stomach like the smell of a cheap stogie." He reached for his suit coat that was draped over the back of a kitchen chair. "Aren't you ready yet, Miggs?"

"All except for putting on my dress. I'll nurse the baby first." She took the baby off the couch and carried her into the dining room. She sat in a rocker by the base-burner, looking like a short-haired, tanned madonna in her blue robe and the baby at her breast.

"Sit down near the stove and rest, Katie Rose," she urged. "You look all shivery and big-eyed."

It had been frightening to witness Dawson's raw hate for Mr. Carmody. And she was fidgety to reach for the telephone on a stand near the door and call

Uncle Brian. Perhaps she had better check on the departure time of planes and trains and buses first.

Miggs's gentle voice reached through her plans, "Remember, Katie Rose, when you were out with Miguel for the eggs? Remember you said it was a happy day for you? What's wrong this time?"

Everything, she thought with a sick feeling. But she answered, "Everything will be fine after tonight," just as Johnny came in the back door.

He stood in the dining room doorway to announce, "Here I am, all shaven and shorn, and Pop Carmody has rolled down his shirt sleeves, put in his cuff links, and put on his coat. Is our little miss well tanked up?"

"I think so. Katie Rose can burp her while I put on my dress."

But Mr. Carmody took over that job. He was still walking the floor, patting and crooning to her, when Johnny and Miggs came down the stairs. Johnny was in a white shirt and dark suit. Miggs wore a changeable copper-colored taffeta that looked at least five years old to Katie Rose. Miggs wore no jewelry except her wrist watch, and comb marks showed in her damp, sun-bleached hair.

Katie Rose said, "Lipstick, Miggs. Let me put it on for you. I always do Mom's because she never gets it in the corners."

Miggs said, "When we come back—and we'll have

to be here by ten-thirty at the latest so I can nurse the baby—we'll make tea. And you tell us what's gone wrong."

Katie Rose blurted out, "Were you always so happy, Miggs?"

"No, Katie Rose, no. When I was your age I was miserable."

"But why, when your mother and father gave you everything?"

Mr. Carmody was now tucking the baby into her bassinet, and Miggs could only murmur, "It's a long story. We'll talk tonight about the torturous teens."

She told Katie Rose about the cold chicken in the icebox, and the strawberries and thick cream for shortcake. Johnny told her not to worry if the baby didn't go right to sleep. "Just jiggle the bassinet a bit." And all the while Mr. Carmody was saying, "Come on, Miggs. Come on, Johnny."

Miggs reached absently for a mink stole which Katie Rose imagined was from her Miggs Carmody days, and pulled it over her shoulders as casually as though it were a wool scarf. Even though the men waited at the back door, she lingered a moment by the bassinet. "She's so tiny, isn't she? This is the first time I've ever gone out in the evening and left her."

"She'll be all right, Miggs. I'll take good care of her."

Miggs raised her hazel eyes to Katie Rose's. She reached over and impulsively kissed the baby-sitter on the cheek. "I know you will, Katie Rose. I feel perfectly safe leaving her with you."

Little Melody didn't go
to sleep at once, but lay in her bassinet kicking and
gurgling. Each time Katie Rose bent over her to pull
the blanket back in place, the baby's dark eyes caught
hers, and her smile was joyous and confiding.

Each time Katie Rose murmured, "You're a
blessed."

But she had phone calls to make. First the airport.
She was told the price of a one-way flight to San Francisco, and that a plane was leaving tonight at eleven-
fifty. She called information at the Union Station.
The next train to San Francisco left at eight-fifteen
in the morning. That wasn't so good, even though the
fare was seventeen dollars cheaper than by air. She
ruled out going by bus when she found that a San

226

Francisco bus left at nine tonight, and there was no other until ten-thirty the next morning.

With this information jotted down, she put in a call to Uncle Brian's apartment. She wondered about telling him why she was leaving Denver and Adams High in such haste. But surely if she told her loyal, redheaded uncle of Mrs. Dujardin's injustice— Surely he would remember his saying, "I'm in your debt, bright angel. If ever you need me, just yell my way."

She would tell him she had thirteen dollars to apply on the fare he wired—ten from her night at Giddy's, and three from her Eva-sitting job. She suddenly remembered something else. He could wire her a *ticket*. She remembered Miguel saying, "Dad wanted to wire me a ticket to come to Alaska for spring vacation, but I told him about Gramps with his leg in a cast and Gran needing me." This would simplify things for Uncle Brian—and for her. She could go directly to the airport instead of Western Union first.

But there was no answer at his apartment. Operator 25 asked if she should try again in twenty minutes. "Yes, please." Uncle Brian must be out to dinner. He'd surely be back soon.

She was too full of plans to do more than eat a piece of chicken and a buttered roll while she walked the floor.

The baby cooed on in the bassinet. Once as Katie

Rose pulled up the blanket, little fingers clutched her thumb. With her free hand she joggled the bassinet. The brown eyes grew heavier and heavier until, with a final flicker of smile, they closed. Gently, Katie Rose extracted her thumb from the rosebud fist, covered the baby, and turned out the dining room light. She tiptoed into the kitchen, carrying the phone, and set it on a chair by the door.

The mongrel dog scratched at the kitchen door and she let him in. Operator 25 was telling her for the third time that there was still no answer on her call, when the door opened and an old man limped in. Old Charley had come over to watch his favorite TV shows.

She wished he hadn't. He asked her if she liked "Brave Men of the West." He wanted to tell her about his old days as a bronco buster. She didn't want to listen to him or his Brave Men, and she didn't want his listening to her when she finally reached Uncle Brian.

She was jittery and restless. She washed her hair so it would be shining clean for her trip. She wished, as she combed it straight, that she had curlers for putting it up. Miggs wasn't the kind to own or bother with them.

Again she wished she hadn't worn the Purdum tennis shoes, old plaid skirt, and slipover to school this morning. She'd look so much better alighting from a plane in pumps and her purple jumper with its frilly blouse.

At twenty-minute intervals Operator 25 rang the phone and reported no answer on the San Francisco call. Nine-twenty. Nine-forty. Each time old Charley gave a start. "Godamighty, sounds like a fire alarm!"

At ten, a voice other than that of the operator answered her breathless hello. A man's voice said, "Katie Rose, it's Mr. Carmody. We've changed our plans a bit. The banquet's over, and Johnny is going home to get you and the baby and bring you to the hotel."

"Oh?"

Yes, Mr. Carmody told her, he had met a photographer at the banquet who was nationally famous for his baby pictures. He was leaving town early in the morning, but Mr. Carmody had his heart set on getting pictures of his grandchild. He wanted Melody's smile captured on paper. "This photographer hasn't time to come out to the farm but there's no reason the baby can't be brought down here. She's always wide awake at ten or ten-thirty for her feeding. Wait a minute."

Miggs's voice came over the wire. "Dad wants to be in the picture, he means." She told Katie Rose she would find a canvas bag on the bathroom door that already held diapers and bottles for warm water. She told her where to find a small white dress with a tucked yoke. "Her cuddle bunny and blankets are there on the clothes rack. Dad says for you to come down to the hotel with the baby and Johnny, and then he'll put you in a taxi to go home. Is that all right with you, Katie Rose?"

"It's fine." Fine? It was perfect. She would be at the Tower. She could phone Uncle Brian from a booth there. She could even buy curlers at the hotel drugstore. When Mr. Carmody put her in a taxi, she would tell the driver to take her to the airport instead of to Hubbell Street.

She scurried about gathering up the baby's belongings. From the TV set came the rat-a-tat of guns that meant the Brave Men of the West were mowing down either Indians or outlaws. She picked up the limp baby and squeezed her into the fleecy bunny suit. She'd wait and zip it up, and fit her head into the hood at the last minute.

Yes, she was a blessed to submit to being wakened and carried out and laid on the couch. She lay there blinking in the light.

Katie Rose had to explain to Charley about the change in plans. He looked out at the snow, and commented briefly, "Snow or no, it won't take Johnny long to whip out here from downtown. He knows every turn in that road."

The phone rang again, and again Katie Rose leaped to answer it. This time it was Johnny, and he sounded tired and disgruntled. "Katie Rose, I'm delayed a bit. I'm here at Curt's station—you know where we stopped for gas this afternoon?—to get a new headlight. My right one just went out on me. Curt doesn't have the right size but his helper says he'll drive down to the Boulevard and get one." He sighed. "This whole picture-taking deal seems cockeyed to me. But when Mr. Carmody gets his heart set on something, a bulldozer is tame compared to him. So, Katie Rose, have her nibs all bundled up and I'll honk, and you come out. It'll save a little time—"

He broke off to say to someone in the office, "That's right, a fifty-watt. And kind of snap it up, will you, because I've got a baby-sitter and a baby waiting to be picked up."

He turned back to the phone. "Is Melody whooping it up, Katie Rose?"

"No, not yet. She's awake but—"

"Don't think she won't. Don't think she doesn't know when it's ten-thirty and chow time. I'll be there soon as I can."

She hung up the phone, checked to see that the baby and bag were in readiness, and then lifted the receiver to dial long distance again. One last try before she left. Hope at last. For she could hear the operator ringing the number and the whirring sound was definitely the "busy" signal.

The dog set up an excited barking and Charley yelled over it, "That must be Johnny turning in the lane."

She hadn't expected him so soon. She could only take time to answer the operator's, "The line is busy. Will you wait?" with "No, I'll have to cancel it now. But I'll call later."

She squirmed into her parka, thinking excitedly, Uncle Brian is home at last. He'll answer when I call from the Tower Hotel. She picked up the baby, wrapping her as if in an envelope in a thick, fleecy blanket. Her parka hood fell back from her head in the process. Heavens, she hated to walk into the swanky Tower with her hair damp and straight, and with bangs like a six-year-old.

"Yeh, here he is," prodded old Charley who had hobbled to the door. "Hurry up now. I'll hold the door open." He held it with one hand, and onto the frantic dog with the other. A small part of her mind was puzzled by the dog's ferocity over Johnny's driving up.

With the blanketed baby in her arms, the canvas bag dangling from one and her own purse from the other, she ran through the snow to the dark blotch of car. The door was open and she plopped herself down in the front seat. She wondered, but vaguely, why the light in the car didn't turn on when the door was open.

She had barely closed the door on her side, when the car fairly leaped off and went rocketing down the rutted lane. Katie Rose busied herself setting the canvas bag at her feet, loosening the fold of blanket over the baby's face and arranging it so she was protected but still had air. She felt in the dark for the soft, warm, little face.

By now the car was turning out of the lane. It didn't turn right toward town, but swerved sharply left.

She looked at Johnny to ask, "Why are you turning this way?"

The man behind the wheel was not Johnny Malone.

On a nervous laugh she said, "Did Johnny send you for me? But you turned the wrong way. You'd better turn back. This road leads to the mountains."

She felt his foot pressing harder on the gas pedal. He threw back his head and laughed harshly. "No, Johnny didn't send me to get you. He and the boss sent me to get a bulb for his headlight. He's still sitting back there waiting for me. Well, he can wait. And old Carmody can sit down there at the Tower and wait too—he can wait till hell freezes over—and see how he likes it."

He reached up and pushed a shapeless hat back on what Katie Rose could see was an unkempt mop of hair, and gave a burst of profanity. The man was Dawson. The man who stood in the farm kitchen a few hours ago and told Carmody he'd be sorry if he didn't give him a job. Then he was the helper at Curt's filling station. "More hindrance than help," Curt had said. He was the one who had been standing there listening to Johnny talking to her on the telephone, the one Johnny had turned to and said, "Yes, a fifty-watt globe, and kind of snap it up, will you, because I've a baby-sitter and baby waiting to be picked up."

She couldn't answer for the clammy fear that gripped her. He went on, "So old big-shot Carmody had a deal to get the baby's picture taken. I heard that young fellow talking about it, and that's when it came to me in a flash: Here's your chance, Dawson, just laid out for you. No, *sir*, if I'd laid awake a year and planned it, it couldn't have worked out prettier." He thumped his knee and gave out a wild, gloating laugh.

He was drunk. No man in his right mind, she realized, would do such a foolhardy thing. He's a knave *and* a fool, as Mr. Carmody said, and that made it all the more fearful. She clutched the baby tight to her.

He went on gloating as the car rocketed along. "So Carmody's son-in-law is sitting back there at that measly gas station expecting me to come back and put his light in and say pretty as you please, 'There you are, sir.' Yeh, and he might even give me a two-bit tip. And old hot-stuff Carmody waiting at the hotel for his precious darling grandchild and you. He doesn't know you're both in for a good, long trip."

He turned his head and looked more closely at her in the dim light from the dashboard. "How old are you? You ain't much more'n a kid yourself. Twelve —maybe thirteen?"

It surprised her. It must be her hair combed straight down, and no make-up, not even lipstick. She started to say, "I'm past sixteen." But some instinct made her say, "Some people think I look older'n twelve and a half." Fear, itself, made her voice thin.

"Twelve and a half, huh! Then you're too young to know what a—" choice profanity "—old Carmody is."

Yet he proceeded to tell her how Carmody had fired him just because he felt like firing someone. She wanted to say, "He gave you three chances. That's more than most men would give you." No, better not antagonize him. Better let him think she was too young to draw conclusions of her own.

"So now I'm pouring it onto him just like he

poured it onto me. I've gone crawling to him for the last time. Now he's got to come crawling to me. Yeh, on his knees, and that's the way I want it." He fumbled for a cigar—one of his cheap stogies—and lit it with a flourish. "No one does me dirt and gets away with it."

He was not only crazed with liquor but with hate and revenge. Katie Rose was not an O'Byrne for nothing. She knew what drink did to a man. On summer vacations in Bannon, she'd heard workmen "spreading the gaff" as her Grandda O'Byrne put it. He'd wink at her and say, "That's whisky talking, child. You can discount ninety-nine percent of it."

The baby was squirming in discomfort, and Katie Rose's shaky hands shifted the burden to her shoulder. She glanced out the car window and spoke out of her surprise, "It isn't snowing now."

"We're climbing out of it. That's what I figured. I figured there'd be no snow in the mountains. Fact is, I've got this whole thing figured out to a fine point. I'm going to stop just this side of Utah. I know a fellow and his wife up there in the hills, and you couldn't find a better hideout. Just this side of Utah, see, so they can't say I crossed a state line." He let out another fiendish guffaw. "Who's going to prove anything on me? I can say you ran out and jumped in my car with the baby. I'll have you do the phoning for me. Yeh, I'm dumb like a fox, I am."

She remembered Uncle Brian's saying once, "There comes a point when drink makes a man think he's powerful smart and the rest of the world is so dumb it's pitiful."

He was asking her, "You ain't scared, are you?"

She answered around the cold lump in her throat as she thought a twelve-year-old would, "Oh no, I guess not."

"As long as you don't try any funny stuff you'll be all right. You better play along with me because I can get plenty rough if you don't. You hear, kid?"

She heard; and she remembered with a shiver the account of the welts on his boys.

They were climbing now. She could feel and sense that mountains were bordering the road on first one side, then the other. The baby in her arms had been stirring in discontent, and she let out a sudden reminding protest.

Dawson's wild talk was easing off. He was not driving so recklessly nor so fast. In a way Katie Rose was sorry, for the hope had flashed through her mind that a road patrol might stop them, and she could cry out, "He's kidnapping us."

At first, numb terror had frozen all thought. The terror was still there, but the wheels of her mind began slowly turning. They must have been riding about an hour on this mountain road. She wished she could see a landmark or road sign that would tell her which road they were on and where it was leading. But he had mentioned Utah, and that was west and north over the pass.

How long had Johnny waited at Curt's station? Surely he had found out by now from old Charley that another car had stopped and she, with Melody, had climbed into it. What were he and Carmody doing about it? On TV shows, the police set up roadblocks. But how could anyone guess which road this abductor was taking?

Was there anything she could do? At this time of night and at this time of year, there was little traffic on the road. Only a few huge trucks passed. Even if she dared call to one for help, its own loud roar would deafen her cry.

The blanketed little Melody, who had been fussing and whimpering and occasionally letting out a wail, now began to cry in earnest. Katie Rose shifted her to her other shoulder, patting the solid little lump of behind under the layers of blanket and cuddle bunny. But the baby cried on in angry and hungry protest, flailing her legs and arms as she did so.

Dawson fidgeted nervously as he drove. The crying persisted and he rasped out, "Shut up that fool kid, can't you?"

The viciousness in his voice added to her terror. *How*, she thought desperately, just *how* could anyone shut up a hungry baby?

Katie Rose laid the baby across her lap and jiggled her knees. For only a brief minute there was a lull and then the wails began again. "She's hungry," she said.

"Too bad about him," Dawson flung out.

She couldn't help correcting him, "She's a little girl."

Not only had Dawson's wild talk run down, but his mood had changed from gloating exultation to edgy nervousness. Katie Rose understood that, too. His drink was wearing thin and with it his high spirits. He ordered, "Feel under your feet there and see if there's a bottle."

She did, and produced one. It had only a swallow left in it and he said as he took it from her, "Christ, I

239

thought there was more than that." He drained it and, letting down the window on his side, hurled it out. The air that rushed in was icy cold.

The baby was screaming now without ceasing, and the man bellowed at her, "You've got to shut him up. Do you think I can put up with a kid screaming in my ear all night long?"

"It's way past her feeding time." Again either reasoning or instinct kept her from saying it was past time for Miggs to nurse her. Maybe if he thought milk would quiet her crying, he would stop and get some. She picked her words carefully and used her little-girl voice, "There's a bottle in this bag I brought, but there isn't any milk in it. I wish we had some milk." And she thought, Go on and scream, Melody, so he'll be driven to stop.

His only answer was an angry mutter around the cigar in his mouth. The baby wailed on, and Katie Rose's thoughts skittered over this possibility and that. She remembered that in a TV movie, a girl captive had written the word "Help" on a match folder she happened to have, and had either dropped it or left it on the counter without her captor noticing.

They were climbing higher and higher. The cold seemed to creep through the car. The baby's cries would come to an exhausted lull and then start again, louder and more insistent. Over it Katie Rose could hear Dawson's mutterings. She could see only his profile in the dim light, and it was mean and ugly.

Even so, she felt in her coat pocket and found the card on which she had written the telephone numbers of the airport, Union Station, and bus depot. She had thrust it into the pocket of her jacket when Johnny telephoned. She had a pencil in her purse. Very stealthily she bent to reach for it.

"What're you doing?" the man yelled.

"I was just getting a handkerchief out of my purse."

"Leave your purse alone. You sit still and keep still, and I wish to God you'd keep that kid still."

Her hand felt a small lump in her skirt pocket. Her lipstick. That was even better, if she could manage without his seeing her. She shifted the crying baby to her left side, letting the blanket fall over her lap and her right hand. She found it took both shaky hands to get the cap off the lipstick and wind out the red stick. The cap dropped from her fumbling fingers, and she looked fearfully at the driver.

Fate seemed to be on her side, for Dawson was peering through the windshield and out his side window at signs that said, "Slow. Road Under Construction." Flares in black pots flickered at the side of the road.

While her fingers wrote "Help!" on the card, and thrust the lipstick back in her pocket, he was muttering something about a new bridge and a widened high-way on both sides of it. Did all his peering out mean that he was looking for a place to stop?

The baby screamed on without ceasing. Dawson was growing more and more driven by it. Katie Rose could have muffled Melody's cries against her shoulder, but she decided against it.

Then she was all attention herself as their lights caught and then lost a few buildings ahead of them, and far to the side of the new highway they were on. It was all she could do to keep from shouting, "There at the side of us! Maybe you can get milk there."

Dawson, the fault-finder. "Look at that. Used to be a few houses here too. People living in them. Then the state decides to put a new highway through here and so the houses are ripped down. All that's left is the store and café. Later on they'll come down too because this new highway is by-passing them."

She sat straight, every nerve taut. The new highway, though under construction, had been made passable. A narrower road, evidently the old one, branched off to go past the attached buildings. Dawson didn't take it. Neither did he stay on the new one, but swung off to one side onto rough crushed rock that had been laid for a wider roadbed. He stopped in a spot that was sheltered by a great pile of gravel and was far from the huddle of buildings. His car was faced away from them and toward the highway he said led to Utah.

A truck was coming up the highway they had taken, but it turned onto the road that led to the low rectangular buildings. Dawson quickly turned out his lights. The truck's strong lights picked out and showed the signs on the buildings. Café and Bar was one; General Store, the other.

Katie Rose craned her neck and looked back with held breath as the truck came to a halt, as its door opened and a workman leaped out and went back to the body of the truck. She gauged the distance between them as about a city block.

Please, Mr. Workman, come within screaming distance of us. You're the first human being I've seen—

Dawson gave his belittling laugh. "Didn't even turn his motor off. Why should he care about using gas? Not when the construction company's paying for it. He's the night man to keep the flares going. Must be about midnight. He's got to fill and light all those pots he brought in."

"Where does he fill them?"

"From tanks back there where they keep tools and supplies."

The workman disappeared into dark limbo near the buildings. Even his truck with the door open and the lights on seemed like a toy truck. Katie Rose shivered as an eerie feeling of unreality swept over her. The near-by road machines were like huge ungainly dinosaurs. The piles of gravel were not piles of gravel but pyramids. This wasn't she, Katie Rose Belford, sitting in a foul-smelling car with a man who right now was craving a drink and whose bravado had changed to brutishness—

Oh, but it *was* real, for the baby she held was sucking hungrily on the knuckle of one of her hands.

"I'm going in the store," Dawson said.

She fumbled for the canvas bag, and tried to keep the urgency out of her voice, "How'd it be if I went in too? Because the milk ought to be warmed—"

The bag was knocked out of her hand on a dreadful oath. "You stay where you are, and don't you try—"

"But I thought—I mean you'll want the bottle for them to fill—"

"The bottle! What kind of a fool do you think I am? Do you think I'm going to give it away that I've got a baby?"

"But you said you didn't want her screaming in your ear all night, and she won't stop unless—"

"He'll stop. I'm getting some knockout drops. From now on he'll be nothing but a wrapped-up lump on the floor of the car."

She forgot her passive role and cried out, "Oh no! I won't let you. She's so little." She could feel the hungry sucking on her fist, and she thought with hot protectiveness, Oh no, you won't! The minute you leave the car, I'm leaping out with the baby. I'll run —where I don't know. I'll hide—where I don't know. I won't just sit here.

Dawson was out of the car and coming around to her side, his feet scrunching in the loose, sharp shale. It was as though he had read her mind, for he said as he yanked open the door on her side, "I'm taking no chances on your leaving. Stick out your feet."

She didn't move, and he grabbed at one foot. Without untying the lace of the tennis shoe, he wrenched it off. The other shoe was tied tighter, and she cried out in pain as he tugged and twisted it. He clawed off her ribbed socks, his vicious nails scraping her flesh.

He walked a short distance from the car, and threw first one shoe and then the other as far as he could. "There now," he gloated, "I guess you'll stay put. These rocks would cut anybody's feet to ribbons."

He banged the car door shut on her and started off, lurching in the loose rock that slithered under his boots. She sat there with the baby, feeling more helpless and caged than if she were locked in. All for naught her writing with lipstick on the card and hoping to make contact with another human being. She could only sit, twisted about in the front seat, and looking through the back window at his menacing figure weaving its way toward those faraway buildings. It was drink he wanted.

She felt a chilling draft on her bare feet. It was coming from the door on the driver's side which hadn't been shut tight. She reached out to close it—

He hadn't taken the keys! In his fury at her "Oh no! I won't let you," he had forgotten. She looked back again at his floundering through the loose shale. He was nearing the buildings. She was almost counting his steps. There, he was on the solid ground of the old road. Now he was opening the door of the Café and Bar—now it had closed behind him.

What she did then was purely reflex. She pushed herself swiftly behind the wheel, depositing the bundle of baby in the spot she vacated. Later she'd take time to make Melody more comfortable. She turned on the motor, the lights, and reached for pedals that felt gritty under her bare feet.

If only she could head back the way they had come! There lay haven and safety. But it would take a deft job of backing and turning to avoid the gravel piles and machinery—and she didn't know how. She had to go straight ahead, even though it took her farther from home. She started, unable to tell which was the roar of the motor and which the pounding of blood in her ears.

Before she had reached the firm ground of the road, she saw in the rear-view mirror the door of the building open and Dawson silhouetted against the light. It was like watching a puppet on a faraway stage gesticulating wildly. No doubt he was yelling profanity along with his fist-shaking. Let him yell and shake his—

Then she saw him running toward the truck. In a sick flash, she remembered that its driver, too, had left the key in the engine. Her bare foot pressed harder on the gas, and the car shot forward around a mountain arm that shut off from view the running man and the waiting truck.

So Dawson meant to chase her down in that commandeered truck. Frantically her eyes searched ahead for a sign of humanity, or a dwelling, or a place to hide. There was nothing but the broad ribbon of road, mountains on one side and a steep declivity on the other.

The blood still pounded in her ears. She kept looking in the rear-view mirror. No car was following her—not yet, anyway. Muffled sounds came from the blanket beside her. But she couldn't take time to straighten out the blanket and settle the baby more comfortably. She could only drive on as fast as she dared.

Once a huge truck loomed up in front of her. She pulled so close to the mountain on her side that one of her tires grazed it. The truck roared by, honking loudly. He was reproaching her, she realized, for not dimming her lights. "I'm not smart enough, Mister," she muttered.

She didn't know how far she had gone when she saw a road leading off from the highway. Small dirt roads like it led to mountain cabins or ski lodges. She'd be safer from Dawson on such a road, and she might locate a human being or a telephone.

She turned onto it. The deep ruts were full of snow which twisted the car's wheels. Before long, her lights picked up rough slab tables with attached benches and stone fireplaces. She had taken a turn-off that led only to picnic grounds. She came to a dead end when she reached a creek.

Now what? She couldn't perch here all night, with the steep creek banks ahead of her. She sat for a long time, clutching the wheel and looking back toward the highway, trying desperately to think. She could see the lights, like fireflies from this distance, of infrequent vehicles going both away from and toward Denver. She could tell the big freight vans by their rear lights.

Suddenly she remembered someone telling of having car trouble on the highway, and of blinking lights for help. "Truck drivers are swell about stopping and giving a hand," that someone had said.

This was her only chance; to get back on the highway and blink her lights at an oncoming truck from Salt Lake way. She practiced it—off, on, off, on. And when a truck stopped, she would pour out her story to its stalwart driver, and he would take her and little Melody to safety.

But she had to back up and turn. Somehow, even though she had passed up Miguel's lessons, she *had* to. She clenched her jaw, murmured to the crying baby in its cocoon, "There now—we'll soon be all right, honey."

She shifted into reverse, pushed the gas pedal. The car shot back. If only she had a flashlight and shoes on her feet, she could get out and see how much space she had for turning. If only she weren't so hedged in by trees, scattered boulders, and all the picnic fixtures. She turned the wheel this way and that as she backed and then went forward. The car seemed to take malicious delight in *not* going the way she meant it to.

She was backing and seeking only to miss a boulder which loomed up on the driver's side. The wheels were now lodged in a rut, and she shoved her foot down hard on the gas— A crash and a rocking jolt! The lights went out, the motor went dead. She opened the car door and peered back. She had banged full force into a stone fireplace.

Hopefully, she turned on the light switch. Nothing. She stepped on the starter. Nothing. Her first thought was of Miguel and his saying, "Learning to back and turn is important."

How right he was!

Katie Rose took her clenched hands off the wheel, and tried to flex her cramped fingers. She was shaking convulsively with cold and fright as she leaned over to rub off some gravel embedded in the soles of her bare feet. They were numb with chill, but when she tried to rub one against the other the left one sent up twinges of pain.

. . . He could have untied that shoe, instead of yanking it off by brute force. She drew certain satisfaction in thinking: But he never once dreamed of my taking off in the car. Him and his knockout drops! . . .

She felt for the whimpering lump of baby and gathered her awkwardly onto her lap. "There now, little sweet, I know you're hungry." She talked out her thoughts to her, "It must be about one o'clock by now. It seems longer than three hours since we left the farm, doesn't it?"

Yes, three hours ago Johnny must have spread the alarm that another car had honked, and she and the baby had gone off in it. "And, Melody," she told the snuffling, sobbing baby, "I'll bet he and your grandfather have got every police car out hunting us." Maybe even now they were passing on the highway. But how could they know she had fled up a rutted road to a desolate picnic grounds?

The night was so black and full of unknown terrors. She said aloud, "There isn't anybody under that picnic table. There are no wild animals this close to civilization." She peered up at the sky where dark clouds hid all but a sliver of moon.

How far was it back to the highway? At least a quarter of a mile. She spoke on to the baby, "I tell you what we'll do. We'll wait here till Dawson has had plenty of time to pass. Maybe by then the moon will come out so I can see where I'm going." Not only the thought of Dawson, but of traversing that rutted, snow-patched road in her bare feet with a hurting ankle and with a baby in her arms, made her cringe closer in the seat.

The baby's crying dwindled and then ceased. The icy mountain coldness pressed up through the floor boards and through a window that didn't shut tight.

The baby needed more warmth. Still holding her, Katie Rose got to her knees and felt in the back of the car. She found an old sheepskin coat. It was gritty and reeked of cigar smoke and Dawson. Even though it was repulsive—like having him near—she tucked it over and around the baby's blanket.

She tried warming her own feet by doubling one under her until it had life in it, and then putting it back and sitting on the other. The trouble was that the warm foot grew cold before the cold foot grew warm. She tried doubling up both and sitting on them. No, her weight hurt the left ankle. But at least the baby was snug. She bent her head and listened to the light, warm breathing.

Sitting out here in the dark and frightening night, she seemed to have left her own identity. She was not Katie Rose Belford, concerned about many things. Her only concern was to guard the baby she held until she could hand her to Miggs and say, "Here she is."

She felt so *detached* from the Katie Rose of Hubbell Street and John Quincy Adams High. Pictures flashed before her mind almost like scenes on a movie screen. She saw a girl in a purple jumper and frilly blouse sitting in Downey's Drug with a dark-haired hero—not a conquering hero, but a confused and dejected one. And, like an onlooker at a film, she thought: Listen to her brag and blow, blow and brag.

She found her stiff lips muttering, "I don't blame the guy for finding another girl."

Another unpleasant picture flashed across her consciousness. It was that same girl clutching Mrs. Dujardin's arm. There she was, blowing and bragging about herself again. The drama teacher was asking, "Did your grandfather ever tell you about their apportioning parts to the Abbey players?"

The girl on the screen was saying no, he never had. But the objective girl, with one bare foot dangling in a cold car, remembered he had—and the very words he used. She had asked Grandda O'Byrne if he had been a leading man at the Abbey Theater. She could even hear his emphatic snort.

"There were no leading men, no stars. That wasn't the idea of it. Take the woman who played the lead in one play. She'd be given the lowliest part in the next— maybe a scrubwoman without a line. And the man who carried the whole show in one play might be cast in the next as a bum leaning against a lamppost. We were a group that loved theater and wanted to learn all there was about it. Once a player gets it into his head that he has to have a big part, he's no good to the director, the other players, or even to himself."

The objective girl in the car winced at the memory of that irate Katie Rose in front of the call board in the greenroom, of her rudeness to Zoe and

Mrs. Dujardin, of her exploding to Jeanie. "I will never set foot in this school again. I will not go home."

And now she longed to set foot in the school again. She longed to go home. The life she had been so rudely jerked out of was now so dear—so painfully dear.

Deep in its swaddling, the baby was making sucking noises. Katie Rose was brought back to the frightening present by a hungry and reproachful wail. She couldn't wait any longer while the moon played hide-and-seek with the black clouds. "All right, my poor starving lamb. We'll start for the highway. Dawson must be far along his way by now."

She put the baby on the seat and buttoned her parka, and stepped out of the car onto the ground. No sooner had the icy grass crunched under her feet than her legs, numb and cramped from long sitting, gave way under her. She pulled herself up by the door handle, held on to it a moment or two. She whacked her legs to bring back the circulation. She thrust her billfold into her pocket, and hooked the baby's canvas bag over her left arm.

She reached then for the bundle of baby, Dawson coat and all.

She could barely locate the road by the white snow in the ruts, and she chose the middle ground between them. Her feet were too numb to mind the prick of pebbles and sharp stubby weeds. It was slow, hobbling going. She hadn't walked far when her left foot twisted on a stone, and her sore ankle sent up such a twinge of pain that again her feet buckled under her, and she dropped to her knees.

She looked back to the dark hulk of car, and one part of her urged, "Go on back to the car. You can never make it to the highway." But another dogged side of her answered, "I've got to."

Laboriously, she struggled to her feet and pushed on. The occasional car lights on the road ahead seemed very little closer. Her eyes watered in the cold, and she had no free hand to wipe them. And you wouldn't think such a small baby would weigh so heavily.

She had stopped for breath when a car with bright lights swept into her vision on the highway. This one did not whisk into view and then disappear as swiftly as the others. It moved slowly, searchingly, while a strong searchlight played over the area. Her heart set up an uneven pounding as she watched it taking the turn off the road she had taken. Now she could see the light, like a Cyclopean eye, in the top of the car. Only police or road patrol cars had those.

She wanted to race toward it, to scream out, "Here we are." But her legs went suddenly wooden.

She couldn't move, not even when the car stopped a short distance from her and she and her burden were caught in its bright light.

Both doors of the car burst open and two men leaped out. One was a highway patrolman. Was it because she was blinded by the glare that she imagined the other was a familiar lanky figure who came running toward her with a shambling gait? But who else would have his shirttail half in and half out under an unzipped jacket—?

She heard his shout, "Petunia, we found you! Didn't I tell you, Sergeant Metcalf, I could find her?"

He was beside her, both arms steadying her as she swayed. "You all right? The baby all right?" he kept demanding.

She could only nod. Words wouldn't come.

"You're not hurt—either of you?" the officer asked.

"We're—fine," she managed.

Patrolman Metcalf, so beautifully uniformed, capped, and booted, so strong and competent with his holster belt sagging over his hip, took one glance at her wan face and blue lips before he took the weight of the baby from her arms. "The car's just a step or two. Can you make it?" he asked.

She didn't have to. Miguel scooped her into his long arms. He put her on her feet at the car's door.

The patrolman was already there and before he could deposit the squirming baby on the back seat, she said, "Wait just a minute." She reached out and pulled that dirty, smelly coat off Melody. She rolled it up tight and gave it a vicious toss into the darkness. "There! Now I feel better."

She explained as they helped her into the back seat, "He took off my shoes—Dawson—and threw them as far as he could. When we stopped back there where all the road-building machinery and the stores are."

Miguel climbed in beside her. "Why'd he do that?"

Through chattering teeth she answered, "He—he—was afraid I'd leave—with the baby—when he went in the store."

Sergeant Metcalf turned from behind the wheel. "Why, that stupid scum. Didn't he figure you could drive a car without them?"

"He never thought I could drive. He thought I was about twelve or thirteen—and so I pretended I was."

"How old are you?"

Miguel answered for her, "She's sixteen."

The patrolman was maneuvering the car about to face the highway. "You've got a lot of what it takes for sixteen."

As she took the baby onto her lap again, he was

radioing in to headquarters, "Metcalf in car 21 reporting. Have kidnapped girl and baby with me. Just off Route 40. Coming right in. Call in all other cars that are looking for them."

How short that rutted road really was! Katie Rose had time only to loosen the baby's blanket when the car turned onto the highway and was skimming along toward Denver.

Miguel fussed over her like a mother hen. He took off his jacket and put it on the floor, wrapping it about her feet. "Don't shiver so, Petunia. Can't you feel how warm the car is?"

"I wrecked Dawson's car," she confessed. "I backed into a rock fireplace and then it just wouldn't start."

"Did the lights go out?" Miguel asked.

"Yes, and the starter wouldn't start."

"Doesn't sound like you wrecked it. Sounds like you popped off the battery cable."

"He started to chase me in a truck. Do you know where he is now? I'll always be afraid of him. He said no one ever did him dirt and got away with it."

The patrolman said, "He didn't get far in the truck. He had an accident." And it was that accident, he told her, and the road patrol reporting it that had narrowed the search for her and the baby. "We tied the kidnapping to this fellow Dawson right away.

But until we located him by the accident, cars were fanning out in all directions."

"How did you know where I was?"

"Your boy friend here figured that out. Nobody saw you leave. But everyone figured you'd make a beeline back to Denver."

Miguel said, "Soon as word came through that Dawson had banged up himself and the truck, I said that if I could find out from the workman how Dawson's car was faced I'd know which direction you went in. I knew you wouldn't be able to back and turn. I told Sergeant Metcalf you'd go straight ahead and that you'd be so scared of that monster you'd turn off on the first road you came to."

All this time the warm car was smoothly covering the miles. They passed the fateful spot where Dawson had stopped. The driver said only, "Things are quieting down here, now," and went speeding on.

Katie Rose had been cold so long. The warmth of the car turned her sick and faint. The lights in the dashboard were doing queer things; they left their place and came toward her, then blurred and faded. Voices also came to her strong, and then blurred. Her ears rang fuzzily.

Patrolman Metcalf was busy on the radio. He

relayed to her and to Miguel that the baby's mother was with Mr. Carmody at the Tower Hotel; that Johnny Malone, following some false clue, was still out on the road leading south to Cherry Springs.

She felt herself swaying forward on the seat, and Miguel's arm tightened around her. "Sergeant, she's about had it," he said. "Can't we drop her off at her house first and then deliver the baby?"

She roused and said with labored precision, "I want to go where Miggs is. I—want—to—give—her —the—baby."

She thought the patrolman said he would see what they could work out, because right then little Melody decided there was little nourishment in Katie Rose's knuckles and protested loudly to the world. The car's speed increased.

Katie Rose roused again to hear Miguel saying, "Turn here, Sergeant Metcalf. There, the house on the corner where all the lights are on. Get as close as you can because Petunia hasn't any shoes."

The car drew up in front. Yes, every light blazed in the house and on the porch. So many cars were parked in front and at the side, the patrol car had to hunt for space.

It had no sooner stopped than the Belford front door opened and people poured out. Katie Rose repeated, "I want to give the baby to Miggs."

Miggs was the first one to reach the car. She was still in her bouffant taffeta dress with a man's suit coat over her shoulders. The light of the car showed the bones under her drawn tanned face.

She reached out her arms and Katie Rose put the crying baby into them, and said, "There!" And on an afterthought, a mumbled, "She's wet—but I—I didn't change her because—"

A flashbulb went off as Miggs said chokily, "Katie Rose, I'll never forget—as long as I live I'll never forget— what you've done—"

A man with a camera plucked at Katie Rose's arm. "Did Dawson threaten you or do you bodily injury? Did he say how much ransom—?" But Mr. Carmody was there, brushing the Press aside. "That's about it, men. You can get the facts from the police. I've already talked to the papers about playing it down for everyone's sake."

Again someone picked up Katie Rose and carried her in. She wasn't even sure who it was until he deposited her in their front hall and she saw Ben's red head. She said irrelevantly, "Oh—Ben. Did someone iron your white jacket this evening?"

She had to cling to the newel post. Her arms, empty of their burden, twitched convulsively. She could see them all, Mother, Stacy, the littles, neighbors, people she didn't know. She looked down at the shabby rug under her feet. It was so beautiful that in spirit she bent and kissed it. The odor of paint smelled so clean, so right.

Her mother was coming toward her with a steaming cup of something, and Katie Rose thought in panic, I can't say anything. I'll break down and babble like an idiot if I do.

With that, someone—it could have been Stacy or Jill—screamed out, "Katie Rose, look at your hands. They're all bloody."

She held up both palsied hands. They were smeared with red, and for a dazed few seconds she could only stare at them in bewilderment. "It's not blood, it's lipstick—indelible lipstick," she said and began to laugh. "See, I wrote with it—on this card—and I got it all over my skirt too because I lost the cap—" She held up the card with the almost indecipherable "Help!" on it.

Mr. Carmody demanded tersely, "Did that man lay a hand on you, child?"

"No, he just took off my shoes—and my socks—and threw them away. But I didn't care—because I never liked those tennis shoes—they had William J. Purdum stamped on them—" She began to laugh so wildly and uncontrollably that she had to hold tighter to the newel post.

Why didn't anyone else think it was funny? What was Jeanie's father, Dr. Kincaid, doing here? And why did he come forward with a glass of water and a white pill in his hand, and say firmly, "Katie Rose, take this."

Why, for that matter, did her own shrieks of laughter turn into great shuddering sobs so that her mother drew her close into her arms, soothing, "There, there, my own—my dear own. You're home now— nothing can harm you. Ben, help me get her up the stairs and to bed."

She heard her own childish wail, "I want to brush my teeth and wash my hair—I don't want to smell like *him*."

A bright sun was shining through the bedroom window when Katie Rose opened her eyes the next morning. She lay for a brief moment, warm and relaxed. And then the whole ugly and frightening memory came back. Dawson. Dawson, who had said, "Nobody does me dirt and gets away with it."

Stacy was already up. Katie Rose remembered that through her heavy, troubled sleep, she had reached out and felt the warm weight beside her and been comforted by it. She looked at the clock on the dressing table. Goodness, nine-forty. Her eyes turned back to the window and the wonderfully bright sun. Today was the first of April and the deadline for turning the story of her life in to Mr. Jacoby.

She threw off the covers and sat up, pushing back her rumpled black hair. A reminiscent shudder went through her. Her hair seemed to hold the smell of stale cigars—yes, and a dank whiskey breath.

Ben rapped on the door and pushed it ajar. "I thought I heard you stirring. We're all waiting for you. Mom said for you not to dress. Here, just slide into your robe."

She looked down at her taped ankle as her feet touched the floor. "I sort of remember Dr. Kincaid fixing my ankle last night," she mused.

"Do you?" Ben was buttoning the robe for her. "You were so beat and sleepy he had to finish it after you were in bed. He stayed to be sure you and the baby had suffered no ill effects from your midnight ride."

"Is the baby all right?"

"Right as rain. Miggs called this morning to tell us. Do you remember Dr. Kincaid telling you that Jeanie had been here until midnight, and then he sent her home? But when we got the word that Miguel and the highway patrol found you, we telephoned and told her."

"I sort of remember. I meant to tell Dr. Kincaid to ask Jeanie to bring my books to school today."

The littles were hovering close to the door, and Matt said, "You sure don't remember very good.

You did tell him about the books and Jeanie is going to."

Katie Rose turned wondering eyes back to Ben. "There's something else. Did I dream it—because I had such weird dreams—that someone came to the door and told Mom and Dr. Kincaid that Dawson was—was—?"

"Dawson was dead," Ben finished for her. "No, you didn't dream it. It was me you heard telling Mom and the doctor. The police phoned to report that he died in the ambulance on the way to the hospital."

She dropped weakly back on the bed. "Dawson is dead," she breathed.

Ben said, his eyes on her white face, "When I told them, Dr. Kincaid said, 'Well, as my Scottish mother would say, that'll save the taxpayers the price of a trial.' And Mr. Carmody said, 'For years that man has been bent on destruction. And now he's destroyed himself.' "

Jill burst out, "You know what happened, Katie Rose? It was the fellow who sets the flares by the side of the road who saw him starting off in his truck. And he yelled at him to stop but Dawson was taking off like a shot out of a gun, he said. And so this fellow threw one of his lighted pots at the windshield because—like he told the police—he thought maybe that'd stop him. It didn't, but they figure it must have blinded him because wham! —he plowed right into a real heavy rock-crusher machine. And that's how—"

"And that's about enough out of you," Ben said. "Go tell Mom and Stacy she's coming down."

It wasn't quite enough out of Jill because she yelled back over her shoulder, "You're going to be surprised, Katie Rose."

"Why are the littles out of school this morning, Ben? And you?"

"Stacy too," he said with a wait-and-see look. "Come on."

They were all waiting at the foot of the stairs. The telephone was ringing, and Brian imparted proudly, "It's rung fifty-two times this morning. Matt and I counted them."

Mother said, "Let it ring for a change. I'm tired of answering it. Lovey, we're all waiting for you to christen the new shower."

Why, of course. This was the first of April, and Leo had said he'd have the new bath ready if he had to bust a G-string. And on that yesterday that seemed so long ago, Mother had said they would be casting ballots to decide—

"But don't you remember, Mom? You said we'd put it to a vote?"

For a minute no one answered, and then Stacy threw her arms around Katie Rose and said, "We didn't have to vote, silly. We just all decided by static consent." (She meant tacit consent.) "We were all so scared and so busy praying and answering the phone— So here, take the scissors and cut the ribbon."

A wide, white ribbon was stretched across the new bathroom door and tied in a bow.

Katie Rose looked at her joyous, enthusiastic family. But they hadn't spent hours with a man poisoned by hate. Didn't they know you couldn't turn off memory like turning off a faucet in either a new bathroom or old? She looked more closely at their faces. They had suffered, too. She could see the ravages of it under her mother's smile. Ben's thin face looked thinner, and Stacy's eyes were red-rimmed and swollen.

Mother's laugh had the catch of a sob. "We let you brush your teeth last night but you were too far gone for any hair washing. But now you can. One of our neighbors brought over her hair dryer so your hair can dry while you eat breakfast."

Katie Rose snipped the wide, white ribbon. She opened the new and newly painted door to be met by a mingled odor of scented soap and paint. Here were Mother's dancing peasants and frolicking sheep on the wall. Here were the shiny porcelain fixtures over which Katie Rose had worried lest a certain caller see them sitting naked in the hall.

Mother said, "Let me lather your hair and then you can rinse it when you take a shower. Somebody even sent this eye mask."

"Mrs. McHarg sent it," Jill enlightened them. "And she says she wears one and never gets even one little drop of soap in *her* eyes."

"Wouldn't you know!" Mother said, and everyone laughed.

When Katie Rose's head was covered with white foam she lifted it and said, "That ought to take away the smell of those cigars he kept chomping." In the filigree mirror above the washbowl, her haunted eyes met her mother's sober ones. "Mom, is it a sin to be—not glad, but relieved to hear that someone is— is—?"

"That Dawson is dead? I felt guilty, too, because I felt the same way. Oh no, love, not any more than if a mad dog had come to an end. The only grief is that no one can feel grief. I keep thinking of his wife and boys who've been hiding from him in terror all these years. . . . Turn around, while I tie on this eye-protector."

She said from the doorway, "Don't hurry, Katie Rose. Mr. Knight called, and I told him you'd said something to Dr. Kincaid about having things to finish up at school today. But Mr. Knight said not to come till you had a good rest. Miguel said he'd get out of French, and drive over after you."

Katie Rose stepped into the murky green dimness of the shower. It took a while of turning knobs to regulate the spray. The shampoo suds on her hair washed off and so did the last clinging reminder of Dawson. She soaped every red smudge of lipstick off her hands. She turned this way and that, feeling the cleansing needle pricks of water.

Mother had said, "There's something so miraculous and heaven-sent about our getting a shower." The shower itself was miraculous. It was like Brian's magic slate he was so fond of showing off. On the slate of her mind Katie Rose had written, "Stacy is a snake in the grass, and I will never forgive her or Bruce." She had written, "Mrs. Dujardin is taking her spite out on me, the old hypocrite."

But now the sheet was lifted and the paper was clear and unsullied. She could even say in a low voice, "Bruce likes Stacy better than me," and it didn't hurt. And, "I didn't get an acting part in the school play," and feel no indignation. Katie Rose had christened the new shower and the new shower had christened her.

She dried herself feeling happy and hungry and

at peace with the world and in a hurry to get back to it.

There was still another surprise. The littles said, "Look what came for you by special messenger while you were taking a bath," and held out a pair of black, low-heeled pumps, and a box of sheer stockings. Mother was on the telephone and she capped the mouthpiece long enough to say, "That Carmody! What a time I've had holding the man down. He wants to give you the sun, moon, and stars."

Brian smiled wisely, "He asked us if we knew what you wanted. And we told him something you always said you did. Only it's going to be a surprise."

The bustle, the solicitude. Stacy put up Katie Rose's dark hair on curlers and fitted on the dryer. Ben was at the stove frying ham and eggs for her. "I cooked two because one was cracked and most of the white had leaked out."

She didn't even resent those cracked Bannon eggs this morning.

In the room they shared at the head of the stairs, Katie Rose and Stacy dressed for school. Katie Rose said, "I don't want to ever wear the clothes I had on last night."

"You never will," Stacy told her. "Mr. Carmody wadded them up and put them in the ashpit. But he found out your size from Mom so I have a hunch you'll never miss them."

Katie Rose reached in the closet for her coral-colored cotton, cut on princess lines, with each gore of the skirt outlined with small white ruffles. She hadn't worn it, or wanted to, since that sunny afternoon she had donned it in anticipation of Bruce's visit, since what she had once thought of as the afternoon of her betrayal.

She didn't think of it that way now. The clock on the dressing table said eleven-thirty, which was the time Miguel said he would come for her. She the time their French class started at Adams and smiled as Stacy zipped it up and thought of how Miguel would say, "I see you're wearing our petunia dress."

He didn't say exactly that. She came down the stairs just as he came in the front door and sang out, " 'The petunias that bloom in the spring, tra-la-la.' Madame said we could skip French today, and Jeanie said she'd be waiting at your locker."

21

Mr. Knight was standing in the doorway of his office when Katie Rose and Miguel walked into John Quincy Adams. The principal stepped up to her and shook hands. "We're all glad to see you, Katie Rose," he said gravely.

Jeanie was waiting at their locker holding her sack of lunch. She, too, regarded Katie Rose with gravity. "The reason I'm not throwing my arms around you and making a big fuss is because Mr. Knight is watching. If you see all your teachers and friends looking at you with awe and loving concern but saying nothing, it's because the whole school has been warned not to."

"You mean the whole school knows about—about last night?"

Miguel answered, "It was on the late TV newscast

that you and the baby had been snatched. And it was on the early morning one that you were both safe and sound. Mr. Knight kept calling last night. He talked to your mom this morning. And so in assembly he said it was one of those unhappy catastrophes with a happy ending. He told us all not to keep reminding you of it—you know, by having you rehash it."

Jeanie handed her her books out of the locker. "Oh, Katie Rose, it must have been terrible."

Katie Rose took the familiar weight of books. "I was so scared," she confessed. "But now—ever since I used the new shower—why, it's only like an awful nightmare you wake up from and see the sun shining."

"Come on, you two," Miguel urged. "The lunch bunch is gathering."

"You go on," Katie Rose said. "I want to see Mrs. Dujardin for a minute."

"I just saw her heading for the stage door of the auditorium," Jeanie told her. She walked a few steps with her and, out of earshot of Miguel, asked, "You didn't get Uncle Brian last evening, did you?"

Katie Rose shook her head. "And it's a blessing I didn't. Because he'd have got the truth out of me. He may be long on blarney, but I realize now—I realized it sitting up there at those dark picnic grounds—that he'd have said, 'I'll have no part of your running away, bright angel.' I'm so glad he didn't answer. How did you know I didn't reach him?"

Jeanie's eyes took on their old twinkle. "He called me early this morning. He said all he got at your house was a busy signal, and he was wild when he caught a bit of the news on his car radio. He wants you to call him collect as soon as you're out of school. He just wants to hear your dear voice, he said."

They laughed together at the thought of Katie Rose making a collect call under circumstances so different from yesterday. And then Jeanie hurried to the lunchroom and Katie Rose went through the stage door.

Mrs. Dujardin was sitting on a corner of her cluttered desk drinking coffee. The black sweater was sliding off her shoulders. She said, "Why, Katie Rose child, I didn't think you'd be at school today."

"I had things to finish up. I wanted to tell you I didn't mean what I said about not taking the square dance part. One of my ankles is a little sore but I'll be able to practice in just a day or two. I hope you didn't give my part to someone else."

"No, Katie Rose, I kept it for you." The black eyes were not aloof today. They had their old warm shine.

Katie Rose blurted out, "I did remember—last night when I was remembering things—what Grandda said about the Abbey players and—and their not wanting anyone to get a star complex—"

"It can be a handicap," the woman put in kindly. "Hadn't you better sit down so as not to put weight on your ankle?" She stood up and pushed out her own desk chair.

"Thanks, Mrs. Dujardin, but I have to go on to the lunchroom. I just wanted to tell you."

The drama teacher patted her fondly on the arm. "I'm glad you did," she said simply.

Katie Rose was on her way to the lunchroom, and trying not to limp, when she saw a boy coming down the hall. Those familiar broad shoulders under a bulky, hand-knit white sweater, and the dark mat of hair so like a lamb's pelt. She waited for the old fluttery-swish under her ribs. There was none. She couldn't believe it.

He was abreast of her now and she said, "Hi there, Bruce."

He stopped and said, "Well hi, Katie Rose. Gee, we were all so worried last night when—" Remembering Mr. Knight's injunction, he broke off with an apologetic smile.

For a brief moment they faced each other in the noisy hall. No, she couldn't believe it. The miraculous shower had even washed the scales from her eyes. No rose-colored aura surrounded him. He was not Mr. Irresistible. For the first time she had no desire to impress him. Because, as Jeanie said, he was merely a good-looking, well-mannered seventeen-year-old boy with beautiful teeth and a dazzling smile who happened to like her sister. Her heart was like a bird set free.

He said, "Better watch that ankle, Katie Rose," and she answered over her shoulder, "Oh, it'll be all right."

She made her way through the odorous din of the lunchroom to the table where her "lunch bunch" was already gathered.

Miguel pulled out her chair for her. "Petunia, not one of us even bit into a sandwich until you came and filled the empty chair." The John-Toms said, "You, with the pansy eyes, we salute you, we love you. We all chipped in and bought you a coke and a slab of chocolate pie as an expression of undying admiration."

George, the polite boy from the Philippines, said with a duck of his head, "And thanksgiving that you are here with us."

June's Mona Lisa half-smile was a whole one for Katie Rose. Deetsy broke out, "Everybody thinks it's crummy because Mrs. Du didn't give you a better part. Nobody blames you for telling her you wouldn't be a dancer in the background."

For only a minute Katie Rose hesitated. "It was my own fault. She didn't think much of my telling her how good I was. I just saw her and told her I wanted to be one of the square dancers. Zoe is lending me her dress with purplish flowers—"

Miguel interrupted, "Eat fast, everybody, or the bell will ring and catch us unfed."

Katie Rose attacked her pie and coke. She looked around at them all. It would sound sappy if she burst out, "I'm so grateful to be back with you all. Maybe I look like the same girl who always sat here, but I'm not. I'm a little bit different."

Fifth-hour study hall was next. Again Miguel and Katie Rose halted by their desks and measured how far the shaft of sunlight pushed through the west window. "It's finally caught up with your elbow," Miguel said.

She put her books on the floor, for she would need her desk space for writing. Again Miguel's whisper reached her from the seat behind, "Hold still for just a minute while I chomp down the last bite of apple."

Again, as on the first of March, Jeanie Kincaid came in late. She handed Mr. Jacoby her detained slip and, sitting down beside Katie Rose, explained in that almost soundless communication they had perfected, *"You're* why I'm late. Mr. Knight noticed you limping and he called my dad. And Dad told me to tell you you needn't humor your ankle but if it got sore and swollen to stay off it."

"It just hurts when I walk," Katie Rose answered, and they both stifled their giggles.

She took the many written pages out of her Prose and Poetry book. She ran her eye over some of her written words:

"My mother is not the typically calm, unruffled Mother-type. She is redheaded and impulsive and tempery, and she plays the piano for a living, and she never follows any household routine or reads books on child psychology as most mothers do."

She read her description of Ben, who scolded and bossed them all. Of Stacy, who was untidy, slap-happy, and did crazy and unbelievable things with words. And the littles, who were always underfoot when you didn't want them, and never at hand when you did. By writing small she had room to add, "But they're the kind of family to make life delightsome."

On the last page she had written, "My heart's desire is to be a star." She scratched out "be a star" and wrote instead, "learn as much as I can about theater."

. . . Sitting there in study hall with her whole mind on the ten pages she must turn in before the bell rang, she had no way of knowing that at that very moment a telephone employee was installing a rose-colored telephone in the room she shared with Stacy. That was the surprise Brian had mentioned this morning.

Nor was that all. Special delivery packages to Miss Katie Rose Belford were arriving at the red brick house on Hubbell. Suit boxes with skirts and sweaters. But it was Dawson's depriving her of shoes that seemed to have stuck in Mr. Carmody's mind. At that very moment Katie Rose's mother was signing for another shoe box and murmuring to herself, "I swear that man must think she's a centipede." . . .

Katie Rose turned through her notebook until she found the mimeographed slip Mr. Jacoby had given them when he assigned his pupils the writing of their autobiography. "A final summing up." And she remembered his earnest "Surely in your sixteen or seventeen years life has taught you some lesson."

And surely those hours with a man made insane by failure, hate, and revenge had taught Katie Rose an unforgettable lesson. She glanced up to find Mr.

Jacoby's eyes on her. He gave her one of his rare smiles.

She began to write fast for the bell would soon be ringing:

"Some people learn by good examples. I didn't. I saw my sister Stacy filling up pages with her Mea culpa, mea culpa *but I still wasn't able to say it. I had to learn from a Horrible Example. I had to hear the Horrible Example blaming somebody else for his misfortunes when he should have blamed himself."*

The first and passing bell rang. She turned back to page one and looked up at Miguel and Jeanie who were waiting for her. "I just have to write the title. Which is right, 'This is I, Katie Rose' or 'This is me, Katie Rose'?"

Miguel answered with his impish chipmunk grin, "Depends on whom you're talking to. To a teacher you'd say, 'This is I.' To me you'd say, 'This is me, Petunia.'"

Jeanie gave her her crinkly smile which was the equivalent of anyone else's laughing out loud. "I gave you your title, remember? 'I Was a Teenage Goose Girl.'"

About the Author

Lenora Mattingly Weber was born in Dawn, Missouri. When she was twelve, her adventurous family set out to homestead on the plains of Colorado. Here, she raised motherless lambs on baby bottles, gentled broncos, and chopped railroad ties into firewood. At the age of sixteen she rode in rodeos and Wild West shows. Her well-loved stories for girls reflect her experiences with her own family. As the mother of six children and as a grandmother, she was well qualified to write of family life. Her love of the outdoors, her interest in community affairs, and her deep understanding of family relationships helped to make her characters as credible as they are memorable.

Mrs. Weber enjoyed horseback riding and swimming. She loved to cook, but her first love was writing.